"Drop the weapon, Liz."

Aaron's normally smooth-as-caramel Southern drawl held a steely edge Liz had never heard before. He'd found her. Anticipated her next move.

He stepped closer, the look in his eyes matching his tone. Just for a second she lost what little bit of hope she still clung to. Did he think she was capable of killing her partner?

"Aaron, you scared me." Her voice shook slightly, her nerves wrecked.

"You need to come with me, Liz," he said quietly.

She swallowed back the betrayal she felt at those words. She wouldn't blame Aaron. He was just doing the job he'd been tasked to do.

"I—I can't do that. I didn't kill my partner, but someone wants you to think that I did."

His face twisted with gut-wrenching pain. "I know you didn't kill him, but running makes you look guilty. I promise we'll figure it out together."

Could she trust him? She was close enough to witness the battle raging in him as they faced each other in a silent standoff.

Mary Alford was inspired to become a writer after reading romantic suspense greats Victoria Holt and Phyllis Whitney. Soon, creating characters and throwing them into dangerous situations that test their faith came naturally for Mary. In 2012 Mary entered the Speed Dating contest hosted by Love Inspired Suspense and later received "the call." Writing for Love Inspired Suspense has been a dream come true for Mary.

Books by Mary Alford

Love Inspired Suspense

Forgotten Past
Rocky Mountain Pursuit
Deadly Memories
Framed for Murder

FRAMED FOR MURDER

MARY ALFORD

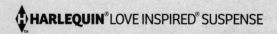
HARLEQUIN® LOVE INSPIRED® SUSPENSE

Recycling programs
for this product may
not exist in your area.

LOVE INSPIRED BOOKS

ISBN-13: 978-0-373-67855-6

Framed for Murder

And there are also many other things which Jesus did,
the which, if they should be written every one,
I suppose that even the world itself could not contain
the books that should be written. Amen.
–*John* 21:25

To my sweet angels, Ava, Kinze and Baylee.
I love you so much.

ONE

You're being set up... The moment Agent Liz Ramirez switched on the burner phone and read the text message, her stomach turned to ice.

The number attached had been blocked. The sender wanted to remain anonymous. That it had come through on her burner phone was disturbing enough. No one knew the number except... Michael.

Her fear for his well-being spiraled. It had been growing most of the day.

She thought about her partner, Michael Harris' earlier depression. When she'd dropped him off at his home after he'd been released from the hospital, she'd sensed something was bothering him even though he refused to talk about it.

Now, standing on his front porch, the same feeling of unease that had followed throughout the day resurfaced.

Liz rang the doorbell. "Michael, are you in there?" she called out when nothing stirred inside.

His car was in the drive. The house looked the same as when she'd left Michael to get some rest, yet the hair standing at full attention on her arms warned her the feeling was neither a figment of her imagination nor a remnant of recent events creeping in.

With the Scorpion team's latest capture of their top terrorist threat known as the Fox, and the weapons he'd supposedly smuggled into the US still missing, the implication hinted at by his second-in-command still troubled Liz. Was someone else involved in the operation? Someone closer than any of them wanted to believe?

She tried his phone once more. She could hear it ringing inside.

Liz reached for the door handle. It opened freely in her hand. As a member of the CIA's elite Scorpion team, Michael would know security was critical. The team had been tasked with bringing down some of the most deadly terrorists operating around the world and because of it, they had enemies everywhere. Michael wouldn't deliberately leave the door unlocked.

With her heart hammering in her chest, she reached for her weapon, eased through the door and into the house.

"Michael, where are you?" The quiet of the house settled around her without answer.

Liz forced herself to breathe as she glanced around the living room. Nothing appeared out of place. His phone lay on the end table as if he'd tossed it there.

"Michael," she called out as she eased to the bedroom. She touched the unmade bed. It was cold. He hadn't been here in a while. A quick search of the closet and adjoining rooms proved fruitless.

That left just one more place. The kitchen. Her stomach chewed with tension. Something was wrong; her heartbeat drummed in warning. It felt as if she were walking through cement as she slowly entered the kitchen and saw it. In an instant, her world crumbled and her worst fear became a reality.

Michael lay sprawled facedown on the tile floor. A pool of drying blood framed part of his head.

Her hand flew to cover her mouth. "Michael," she said in a broken voice then dropped to her knees next to him. He was cold to the touch. Rigor mortis hadn't yet set in. A single gunshot wound to his right temple confirmed the method of death. But the murder weapon was nowhere in sight.

Bile rose in her throat and she sucked in handfuls of breaths before it finally subsided. She couldn't wrap her head around the truth staring her in the face. Michael had been murdered.

Tears filled her eyes, spilled over and soaked her jeans, yet she was powerless to stop them. The man who'd become like a brother to her was gone and she couldn't have felt guiltier.

Since they'd started working together a little more than a year earlier, she and Michael had just clicked. They had the same sense of humor. Liked the same type of action movies, and when they worked in the field, they could almost anticipate each other's moves. That's how she'd known something was wrong with her partner. And yet she'd ignored the warning signals.

Aaron. She needed to let Agent Aaron Foster know what had happened. Time was critical. As field commander of the CIA's elite eight-member Scorpion team, it was Aaron's job to monitor terrorist activity and prevent the recently stolen weapons from falling into the wrong hands. There was little doubt in Liz's mind that Michael's death was related to the Scorpion's capture of the Fox.

She and Aaron had grown close through the years and Liz trusted him with her life. He was a natural born leader and a good man. She respected him like crazy, even though from time to time, they butted heads.

Aaron answered on first ring. "Liz? Are you okay?" The lateness of the hour was proof enough that she wasn't calling to chat.

"No, I'm not. It's Michael…" She stopped when her voice threatened to crack. "Aaron, he's been murdered."

The silence that followed her declaration confirmed the magnitude of the news. Aaron was just as shocked as she had been.

"How? When?" His broken questions were heavy with emotion. Aaron loved Michael as well. Everyone on the close-knit team did.

Liz stuffed down her feelings. She needed to do this as a professional. Michael deserved her best.

"A gunshot wound to the head," she said quietly. "He was killed at close range. From the size of the entry wound, I'd say it was a Glock."

"Are you in danger?" Aaron asked with his concern for her safety intensifying his voice. Their friendship was just as important to him as it was to her. She struggled to stay focused. "No, he's been dead for a while. Whomever did this is long gone."

"I'm on my way. I'll call in Gavin and Alex. We'll be there soon."

She ended the call without answering and stared at the man that she'd shared so many good moments with.

"I'm sorry, Michael. So sorry I wasn't there for you," she whispered and meant it as she scrubbed tears from her face and got to her feet.

Michael's house had now become a crime scene and she had to tread carefully. She'd unknowingly contaminated the door handle by entering the house. It stood to reason that the killer would have touched it at some point. The door had been unlocked.

Using her shirt as protection, she grabbed his phone and checked the outgoing calls. Michael hadn't called anyone in days. Hers were the only incoming today. Had she been the last person to see him alive until the killer arrived?

She thought about his strange behavior after she'd picked him up at the hospital. Was it all due to his near-death experience? She and Michael had been forced at gunpoint into a chopper by the Fox. They both could have died when it crashed to the ground outside a small town in Pennsylvania two weeks earlier. She'd suffered a fractured wrist, a few bruised ribs and some cuts and scrapes. Her injuries hadn't been nearly as severe as Michael's. For a while they weren't sure Michael would make it.

After he was cleared, the doctor had wanted Michael to go straight home and rest, but Michael had insisted on visiting Sam Lansford in prison first.

It had been unthinkable that someone the team all knew and trusted had turned out to be the Fox. When their chopper had crashed, Sam and several of his men had been captured. The team had immediately transported their prisoners to the Scorpion headquarters outside of Painted Rock, Colorado, for interrogation. The weapons Sam had smuggled into the country were still unaccounted for and they needed to find them as soon as possible.

Still, Liz didn't understand why Michael had insisted on seeing Sam. Once the two had faced off, there had been no words exchanged between them.

She glanced around the living room, seeing things through different eyes than when she'd first entered. There was no sign of a break-in. Had Michael known his killer?

One of the cushions on the sofa caught her attention. It was visibly out of place as if something were tucked under it. Liz carefully eased it up and found a large manila envelope stuffed there haphazardly. Her name had been hastily scribbled across the front of it in Michael's handwriting. But it was the next line written there that was the most alarming.

For Your Eyes Only!

Dread wrapped itself snugly around her shoulders. What was Michael trying to tell her that only she could witness? Before she had the chance to open the envelope, headlights flashed across the front of the house.

Liz shoved the envelope in her purse and hurried to the window. She parted the curtains, expecting it to be Aaron. Michael's place was at the end of a sparsely populated cul-de-sac. A car had pulled into the drive and flipped its lights on bright.

She shielded her eyes and managed to get a better look at the vehicle. It looked like the same car that had Michael spooked earlier when she'd driven him home after that strange visit with Sam.

Once they'd turned onto his street, Liz had caught a glimpse of a car behind them. She didn't think anything of it until she saw how Michael had reacted. She'd asked if he knew the person, but he'd denied it.

Liz rushed from the house with her weapon drawn as the car quickly reversed and headed down the street picking up speed along the way. The license plate had been removed.

While the shock of realizing it was the same car as before and that someone had gone to great lengths to hide their identity froze her in place, two additional sets of headlights came down the usually quiet street. Liz squinted through the blinding lights and was able to identify Aaron's SUV. Aaron pulled up beside her. "Did something else happen?" he asked as if reading her thoughts.

She quickly nodded. "I'm pretty sure the car that just passed you was here earlier today when I brought Michael home."

Aaron got out of the SUV and hurried to the truck behind him. "See if you can catch up with the car we just passed. They might be involved."

The driver of the truck, Alex Booth, nodded, put the truck in Reverse and made a quick U-turn before flooring the gas.

Aaron came back to her. Liz knew he could see that she was still shaking in reaction to finding

Michael and to seeing the suspicious car. "Are you okay?" he asked in that serious Southern drawl of his that was always so charming. Now it was laced with worry.

It was so like Aaron to be concerned about her, especially after she and Michael had barely escaped death. He'd always been there for her whenever she needed to talk. Strong. Caring. A true man of valor. She'd often wondered why someone as handsome and as captivating as Aaron was still single.

He ran a careless hand through his chestnut hair before those intense midnight-blue eyes focused on her and just for a second, she lost her train of thought.

"I'm okay," she managed.

Aaron had been tasked with heading up the critical investigation into how someone as close to the Scorpions as Sam Lansford could turn out to be the Fox. As a former CIA agent himself, Sam had quit the Agency to go into business for himself as a hostage retrieval agent. On several occasions, Sam had provided the team with useful information that had led to the capture of some very dangerous people. They'd all thought they knew him. They'd been wrong.

The team had been trying to bring down the Fox and his weapons-smuggling activities for more than seven years. No one expected the terrorist to be someone they all knew.

Yet even with the pressure for answers so great and the guns Sam smuggled out of Afghanistan still missing, Aaron had found time to check on her when Liz's injuries had her sidelined. That was just his way.

He glanced up at the house, his expression solemn. "Take me through what happened. Why are you here so late anyway?" he asked curiously before stepping up on the porch. Was there something accusatory in his tone or was the outcome of the day playing tricks on her?

"I was worried about Michael. I'd been trying to reach him most of the afternoon." She followed him up the steps to the porch. "Since the accident, he wasn't himself. I knew something was troubling him, but he didn't say what."

Aaron nodded. "I noticed it as well. What did you find when you arrived?"

"Nothing out of the ordinary at first, until I tried the door. It was unlocked. I went inside, searched the place and…" She snatched a much-needed breath. "Found him in the kitchen."

Aaron took her hand and squeezed it. "I'm sorry," he murmured with sincerity.

From this day forward, they both knew nothing would ever be the same for her. She'd lost someone else she cared about to an unknown enemy. She still mourned the loss of her husband Eric who had been taken from her far too soon. And now Michael was gone. She considered him family.

Liz waited in the living room while Aaron examined the murder scene. A few minutes later, Alex and Gavin returned from the hunt.

Alex Booth and Gavin Dalton had been with the Scorpions since its inception. They were the best of the best and she was glad they were on her side.

"No sign of the car," Alex told Aaron when he came into the room.

"There's no murder weapon either, but my guess is it was a Glock. The perp must have taken it with him." Aaron nodded to Alex. "Search the place. Maybe we'll get a lead. Call in the local police to canvass the area." He turned back to Liz. "What's your theory here? You knew him better than any of us."

She glanced through to the kitchen where Michael's body lay and tried to hold back the emotions. "I think he must have known his killer. There's no sign of a forced entry or a struggle." She hesitated briefly and then voiced her thoughts aloud. "Aaron, we need to talk to Sam right away. If anyone knows what happened here tonight, it's the man who almost took Michael's life once before."

Aaron drove to the secure prison inside Scorpion headquarters where Sam Lansford had been held since his release from the hospital. Aaron's thoughts were working overtime trying to make sense of their fallen comrade's death.

As much as he wanted to believe Sam was behind Michael's death, too many things didn't add up for it to be so. The biggest being how would Sam have managed to order the murder in the first place?

The capture of the Fox was big. The CIA hadn't taken any chances that Sam might escape. He'd been heavily guarded at the hospital. When he was transferred to his prison cell, a state-of-the-art security system watched his every move twenty-four hours a day. No one got in or out of the compound or the prison without a passkey that was only issued to Scorpion team members.

"What I don't understand is how did he accomplish the hit?" Aaron asked because he couldn't make it make sense in his head. As his second-in-command, Liz had a way of cutting through the clutter.

She turned in her seat. "I beg your pardon?" She'd clearly been lost in her own thoughts.

Aaron noticed the exhaustion around her eyes. The way she cradled her fractured wrist close to her body. Even though it had been two weeks since the crash, he could tell it still hurt like crazy. He had no doubt her bruised ribs were giving her grief as well, yet Liz wasn't one to complain. She'd soldier through the pain, do what needed to be done to solve her partner's murder.

He smiled gently and asked, "How are you holding up?" He nodded toward her wrist and watched as she swallowed visibly and then quickly dismissed the severity of her injuries.

"I'm fine, Aaron. Don't worry about me. I want to help."

He knew her dedication all too well, but that didn't keep him from worrying about her. She was more than a colleague—she was his friend.

Liz was the kindest and most generous person he knew. It never ceased to amaze him that she hadn't let her personal tragedy turn her bitter. She'd been devastated when her husband, and fellow CIA agent, had died while on mission five years ago, yet she'd kept going. Fighting the same causes Eric had battled.

"What were you saying earlier?" she prompted in an unsteady voice when he continued to watch her carefully, getting lost in her expressive eyes.

Aaron cleared his throat and focused ahead. "I was just wondering, if Sam did order the hit on Michael, how he made it happen. He's been guarded since his capture. There have been no visitors."

She considered it. "But if not Sam then who?" She shook her head. "This has to have something to do with the missing weapons."

In his mind, there was little doubt. The team may have captured the Fox, but the guns he'd smuggled into the US from Afghanistan were still MIA.

"Maybe Sam's organization is bigger than we thought. We have no idea how many people work for him." They'd only just begun to dig into Sam's background and so far, it was like peeling away the layers of an onion. There were more lies than truths.

Aaron pulled up to the security gate outside the compound and waved his passkey in front of it. Once they'd cleared the gate, he drove the short distance to the prison.

The moment they entered the section where Sam was held, Aaron knew something was dreadfully wrong. Sam's cell door stood slightly ajar.

He drew his weapon and motioned to the open door. Liz saw and quickly followed his lead.

Aaron pointed to his right and she quietly began searching that section while he did the same.

On this end of the prison, there were only five cells in addition to Sam's. Aaron eased to the open cell. Sam lay slumped on his cot staring sightless at the ceiling. One arm hanging at an odd angle. There was little doubt, he was dead.

Aaron stared at the lifeless body, trying to grasp the reality of what had happened. He couldn't believe it. There was no indication that Sam had taken his own life. No real sign of a struggle and yet someone had murdered him. Aaron's thoughts flew in a dozen different directions. With Sam gone, what did that mean for locating the missing weapons and bringing Michael's killer to justice? Would they ever know the truth behind any of it?

While he tried to process the scene, Aaron couldn't understand how someone had gotten into such a secure location in the first place. He recalled the implication from Sam's second-in-command about someone from the Scorpion team being dirty. Had one of their own team members taken Sam's life? Impossible. Aaron searched the rest of the empty cells, then stopped next to the ones holding members of Sam's team who had been captured.

"What happened here tonight?" he demanded of the first prisoner, knowing full well none of the men captured would cooperate. They hadn't said so much as a handful of words since being taken prisoner.

With nothing but glaring silence coming from the men, frustrated, Aaron went back to Sam's cell. They needed to find out what happened here quickly because there was no way the two murders weren't connected.

He looked up expectantly when Liz returned.

She shook her head, confirming what he knew in his heart. "Whoever did this is gone. Just like at Michael's place. Did Sam's men give you anything?"

"They're not talking." Aaron felt for a pulse,

not expecting one. "I'd say he's been dead several hours. Rigor has just begun to set in."

There were no signs of an injury. Aaron rolled Sam's sleeve up. "There's a needle mark on his arm. He was obviously injected with something deadly," he confirmed while still reeling from the impossible.

"Both Sam and Michael had to be killed within hours of each other," Liz pointed out.

Aaron's gaze locked with hers. "That's right. There are video cameras in each of the cells. Whoever killed Sam has to be on the tape," he told her.

They hurried to the command center and Aaron brought up the video for Sam's cell. The time-stamp appeared to be a few hours earlier. The person who entered the prison was heavily disguised. Dressed entirely in black and wearing a heavy jacket and gloves, their face was almost completely covered with a ski mask with the exception of their eyes. He zoomed in closer, but the feed became grainy.

Aaron pulled up the entry log on the computer. It showed every single entry into the compound as well as which secure passkey was used. What he saw there was most alarming.

The passkey used to enter both the compound and the prison before Sam's death was Liz's. He stared at her in disbelief, unable to digest what was in plain sight.

Each key had a sensor device in it so that when used, that particular Scorpion member was identified as the user. It couldn't be faked. There was no mistaking it was Liz's key. The only question: How?

Her clear emerald-green eyes filled with worry as she shook her head. "No, that's not possible." He'd never seen her look so frightened before. He resisted the urge to take her in his arms and reassure her everything was going to be okay. Since his former girlfriend Beth's betrayal, he hadn't been able to let himself get too close to another woman. He'd loved Beth so much and yet she'd used him, and in the process she'd destroyed his ability to trust his heart to another. Instead, he kept himself buried in work.

Liz tossed her raven braid off her shoulder. She appeared so vulnerable right now, and yet her fragile beauty was deceiving. As a highly decorated agent, he couldn't think of anyone else he'd want to have his back.

"It wasn't me, Aaron," she said in a shaky voice. "I promise I didn't do this."

But if not her, then who? Someone had used her passkey to enter the prison and kill Sam. As much as he wanted to believe her, there was no denying the evidence certainly made her look guilty.

"I don't think you killed Sam," he reassured her because he knew Liz. They'd become close while working together and he'd witnessed time and again that her faith in God was as unshakable as her valor. She didn't kill Sam or Michael, but clearly someone was trying to make them believe she had.

"When was the last time you used your passkey?" he asked, hoping there was some innocent explanation. Maybe she'd lost it. Had it stolen?

She didn't hesitate. "This morning when I left the compound with Michael."

"Where is it now?" he prompted.

"In my purse. Aaron?"

"Go get it," he interrupted and watched as she flinched at the hard edge in his tone.

She stared at him for a second then hurried away and he regretted the way his words had sounded.

When she came back with her purse, he saw the truth on her face even before she said the words.

"It's not there," she said and shook her head. "I have no idea where it is."

Aaron tried to squash the dread growing inside of him. "I need you to account for your time today, Liz," he told her and hated that the request sounded like an interrogation.

She never broke eye contact. "After we left here, I took Michael home and made lunch. I hung out with him for a while and then I left him to rest."

"What time was that? Where did you go afterward?" he asked because they needed to create a timeline before he could her to rule her out as a suspect.

"I left around two. Then I ran some errands and went for a long walk."

All things that couldn't be accounted for unless she'd purchased something along the way.

"What type of errands?" he pushed and couldn't keep the urgency from his tone.

"Aaron, you're scaring me," she breathed the words out.

His heart went out to her but he needed answers now. "I know and I'm sorry." He shook his head. "Answer the question, Liz."

She struggled to bring her thoughts together. "As I said, I left Michael's house around two because he insisted. I didn't want to leave him, but he told me he was tired and wanted to rest. He promised me he'd be okay. He told me he'd call me when he woke up."

"What did you do first after you left Michael?" he prompted and he watched as she swallowed visibly.

"I went for a drive to clear my head then I stopped by the library in town. After that, I got coffee. Hung out a while, and then drove to the trailhead at the base of Painted Rock Mountain. The view there is beautiful and I go there to think. I was there until late. Then…" She hesitated long enough to capture his full attention. "Then when

I didn't hear from Michael, I went to his house. And you know the rest."

None of her earlier moves could be documented fully, which meant she could have had time to murder Sam and then Michael. It didn't look good and he needed to conduct the investigation by the book. He'd have the library and the coffee shop checked. Maybe someone would remember her being there.

"Liz, I need you to go home. Now. You know you can't be part of this."

There was no mistaking the hurt written on her face. "Aaron…"

"Like it or not, you're a suspect because of the passkey and you were the last person to see Michael alive," he said gently. "Take my SUV. Go home and don't talk to anyone until you hear from me." He dug in his pocket and handed her the keys and then walked outside with her.

It was hard to associate the lost expression on her face with the competent agent he knew Liz to be.

"Aaron, you believe me, don't you?" she asked with a hint of desperation in her tone.

He stopped next to the SUV, squeezed her shoulder and tried his best to assure her. "Of course I do. We'll get to the bottom of this. There has to be another explanation we're missing. I'm calling the team in and I'll have Reyna get here as soon as she's finished at Michael's. In the meantime, go home. I'll call you the minute I know anything."

Aaron waited as she reluctantly left the prison. Then he went back inside and called Alex Booth.

"Reyna just left. We're wrapping up here. I called in the local police department as you asked. They're canvassing the area now," Alex said, assuming the reason for Aaron's call.

"Let Gavin finish there. We have a much bigger problem," Aaron said, his tone brittle. He stared down at the lifeless body of the man who had caused so much pain. "Sam's dead." He briefly explained the crime scene.

Stunned, Alex audibly sucked in a breath. "I'm on my way."

"Good. I'll see you soon." Aaron disconnected the call. He knew how bad this looked for Liz, but what he couldn't understand was why she of all people was being targeted.

Agent Alex Booth arrived within minutes of the call. "Reyna's right behind me."

Reyna Bradford was the wife of the base commander, Jase Bradford. As a doctor, Reyna had willingly agreed to head up the medical team for the Scorpions. Reyna was highly skilled and had proven to be a huge asset.

"How did someone get into this secured prison in the first place?" Alex asked in disbelief. When Aaron didn't answer right away, he prompted, "There's more."

"Yes," Aaron said. "It appears someone used Liz's passkey. I've been unable to determine their identity, as the person was covered from head to toe. Whoever did this had a working knowledge of our security system. They must have hacked their way into it."

"Unbelievable. Where is Liz?" Alex asked without thinking.

"I sent her home. She can't be part of the investigation."

Alex shook his head. "I can't see Liz mixed up in this."

Aaron certainly didn't either. "No, but we can't afford to dismiss the evidence in front of us. We need to do this by the book, Alex. Call in the crime scene unit. We need something else to go on other than Liz's passkey. Without Sam's help, we may never know where the missing weapons disappeared to or what the plan was for them. An attack could be imminent."

When Reyna arrived she went straight in to examine the body. It didn't take her long to come to the same conclusion as Aaron. "I have to agree with you, this was obviously something fast acting. The murderer would want to ensure Sam was dead before he left and he couldn't stick around long. I'll know more once I have the body at the lab, but I'm guessing he was killed before Michael."

The killer had somehow gotten Liz's passkey,

then come here to murder Sam. From the video surveillance tape, it appeared Sam had been sleeping when the person entered his cell. When the needle was injected into his arm, he'd woken up, attempted to get up, but was too disoriented. It didn't take long for the poison to do its job. Sam never had a chance.

There was no evidence that anyone had been there with the killer. It was obvious they'd wanted the team to witness the murder. But for what end? Aaron had studied the footage carefully hoping for clarity. The killer was tall and slim built. It certainly could be a woman. He leaned in closer—even though the tape was grainy, he was just able to make out the color of the perpetrator's eyes. They appeared green...like Liz's. He quickly shoved that thought aside.

"Thanks, Reyna," Aaron said with appreciation. Reyna had been an amazing contribution to the team and she and her husband, Jase Bradford, were good friends to Aaron.

Once the crime scene unit arrived, Aaron knew what he had to do even though he dreaded it. Still, it would be best if it came from him. After the director found out about Sam's murder it wouldn't be long before he pulled the case from the team entirely. Aaron couldn't let that happen. They needed answers and they needed them now.

He took Alex aside. "Let me know the minute you have anything. I need to go speak with Liz."

Just saying the words made him feel as if he'd betrayed her.

Alex patted his shoulder. "I know this is hard, but we'll find out what's really going on. It's only a matter of time."

Aaron forced a smile. He sure hoped Alex was right. They needed something, anything that would help clear Liz's name, because he wasn't about to let someone he cared about get framed for a crime she didn't commit.

TWO

The moment she opened the door, Liz knew someone had been in her cabin.

Liz reached for her weapon and eased inside. At first glance, nothing appeared out of place. The quiet of the cabin settled around her. A quick search yielded nothing to back up the feeling.

She glanced down at the envelope in her hand. *For Your Eyes Only!*

The sense of someone watching her permeated every molecule of her body. Was she simply being paranoid?

Liz blew out a shaky breath, killed the lights and parted the living room curtains. Nothing moved in the early morning world outside.

You're being set up... The message from the unknown number had troubled her, though at the time, she hadn't understood its meaning. And in the chaos that had ensued after discovering Michael was dead, Liz had forgotten to mention the text to Aaron.

She grabbed her burner phone again and typed a message to the mystery person.

Who are you? How did you know Michael was dead?

As she stared at the phone, willing an answer to come through, the blank screen in front of her seemed to confirm her suspicions. There was no way the texter could know about her partner's death if he wasn't somehow involved.

Liz struggled to make sense of what had happened in less than twenty-four hours. There had to be something more in the works here than what the team had originally believed. This went much deeper than Sam and his deadly schemes.

Through all the unanswered questions, one thing crystallized. She had now become the number one suspect in Michael's murder. If she let herself be taken into custody, she had a feeling she wouldn't walk out of the prison alive.

Yet if she stayed, with all the evidence mounting against her, Aaron wouldn't have a choice but to bring her in. She couldn't bear the thought of him thinking she was guilty. His friendship had come to mean so much to her.

Either way, time was running out on her freedom and possibly her life, so Liz hurried to her bedroom and stuffed as many things as she could into a backpack, then she went to her closet. The box that held her spare weapon was on the top shelf. Liz felt around until she'd found it. Right away she knew something was wrong. The box's lid was open. Her Glock was gone.

She was almost positive Michael had been killed with the same caliber gun.

It was as if someone was carefully orchestrating her downfall.

Liz dropped her personal cell phone on the kitchen table. If she took it with her, they'd be able to trace her movements. Instead, she grabbed the burner phone and her regulation gun along with the envelope and backpack and headed out the back door.

Leaving headquarters presented another set of problems. She wouldn't get far in Aaron's vehicle. They'd be watching for it. She had one other option.

Don Warren, the ranch's caretaker, kept a work truck close by in one of the old barns. He let every team member use it whenever they needed. If she could reach the barn, it would at least buy her some time, but after that she'd need to find another means of transportation. As soon as the team discovered she'd taken the truck, they'd be on the lookout for it.

She recalled Michael kept an old Jeep stored on the property he leased for hunting, which was adjacent to Aaron's ranch. She'd been to the place once, but had no idea if the Jeep's plates were even current or if it was in working order, but if she could make it there, she'd have a fighting chance of blending in with her surroundings. Jeeps were commonplace here in the mountains.

Liz cracked the back door and listened. Nothing but silence. It wouldn't last. Aaron would be coming for her soon.

"I'm sorry," she whispered for him and then slipped out into the cover of night.

The evening was filled with thousands of stars. It was one of the things she loved about the wide-open ranch. Not a city light could be seen for miles.

Liz rushed to the storage barn that held Warren's old truck. The keys hung in the ignition still. Don kept his passkey secured underneath the driver's seat. Liz fired the tired old vehicle up and eased toward the back entrance of the compound knowing full well the noise would carry. Hopefully, no one was around to hear it. When she reached the gate, she swiped the key and the gate slowly opened.

"Come on, come on," she whispered with urgency while keeping a careful eye behind her.

The gate finally opened enough to allow the truck to pass through. Once she'd cleared it, she floored the gas pedal.

It was a good ten-minute drive to Michael's hunting cabin under the best of conditions. Running for her freedom and constantly checking the rearview mirror expecting trouble made those ten minutes feel like a lifetime.

Once she reached Michael's property, a single strand of barbed wire was all that kept curious onlookers away. Liz flipped the truck lights on bright and got out. A sense of being watched made her reach for the night vision binoculars she'd shoved in her bag last-minute. She scanned the surrounding area expecting someone to have followed her. She felt hunted and she had no idea who was coming after her. But nothing beyond a few animals searching for food stirred the quiet of the early morning.

Discovering her backup weapon was missing felt like the final nail had been driven into her coffin. She had no doubt the Glock would turn up eventually and be matched to Michael's murder weapon and then Aaron wouldn't have a choice. He'd have to take her into custody and she couldn't allow that to happen. If she did, she wouldn't leave prison alive.

With her freedom slipping away, there was only one option left. Run.

Liz undid the makeshift gate leading to Michael's cabin. The grown-up path that served as a road didn't appear to have seen any traffic in a long time. Still, if she wanted to stay under the radar, she'd have to find a place to hide Don's truck.

Once she'd cleared her name and the real killer

was in custody, she'd let Don know where she'd left the truck.

Liz relocked the gate and eased down the path. Overgrown weeds slapped at the truck's undercarriage. After a series of double-back bends, the headlights found Michael's one-room cabin. Tucked in close to the side of the place, his primer gray–colored Jeep was parked under a ponderosa pine.

Nothing about the cabin or the wreck of a Jeep was encouraging. What if the battery had drained due to the cold weather and lack of use? She didn't even know if it was in working order.

As hard as she tried to shut out her worries, she couldn't. She had no idea who was trying to set her up. What if the text message was sent to throw her off and get her out in the open and unprotected? The real killer could be waiting inside the cabin right now.

Liz closed her eyes and prayed fervently, then let God have her worries. She'd need a level head to make it through this thing alive. She couldn't afford to fall apart now.

She parked the truck some distance from the cabin in the shelter of a grove of aspens and peered out the window at the desolate surroundings. A shiver sped up her spine.

Michael told her once that he'd grown up hunting and fishing in Montana. He spoke fondly of his father who had passed away when he was a teen. Yet whenever she'd asked more about his family or his past, his answers were vague. She sensed that his childhood might have been troubled, so she'd let it go. Now she wished she'd been more persistent.

The envelope she'd found at his place called out to her from the passenger seat.

As much as she trusted Aaron with her life, she had to know what was in that envelope before she told him about it. What if something in there implicated her?

Desperate for answers, she ripped it open. A key fell out onto her hand. She turned it over. It appeared to be a house key, but what did it fit? Michael's hunting cabin didn't have a lock. He said he kept it secure by propping a chair in front of the door.

More confused than ever, she pulled out the single piece of paper left inside. It contained a rudimentary map and directions to a remote cabin near Black Bear, Alaska, where Michael went salmon fishing. But it was what was scribbled in the note beneath the map that was most alarming. From the handwriting she could tell Michael had written it in a hurry.

Liz, I'm so sorry. Please forgive me. If you're reading this note, then I'm probably dead and you could be next...

Please forgive me. Tears filled her eyes. What had Michael done?

Go to the cabin in Black Bear. Everything will be explained when you get there. Call Rick Evans. He's a friend and he can fly you to Black Bear. You can trust him. Rick operates out of a private airstrip near Talkeetna, Alaska. Once you reach Black Bear, talk to a woman by the name of Jessie Chena who can get you to the cabin. I've hidden a fireproof box filled with evidence at the cabin. Get there and make sure you don't tell anyone from the team where you're going.

Both Jessie and Rick's phone numbers were written at the bottom of the note.

Don't tell anyone from the team where you're going.

Why hadn't Michael trusted his own team?

Under the best of conditions, Talkeetna, Alaska, was a fifty-six-hour drive from Colorado. Running for her life in a vehicle that was questionable at best, she'd be forced to take as many back roads as possible, which meant the drive would take even longer. Flying was out of the question. She wouldn't make it through the first security check.

With her heart in her throat, she eased from the truck. She hadn't felt this alone since learning Eric had been killed while on that final mission for the

CIA. The days following his death had been filled with crippling grief and long, lonely nights. The pain almost physical.

Now, every little noise had her jumping, expecting the enemy. Aaron. The team she'd vowed to protect had now become her enemy and it was a bitter pill to swallow.

She'd covered only a handful of steps when a noise behind her grabbed her full attention. It sounded like…a footstep on the creaky porch. Someone was here.

Liz whirled with her weapon drawn. "Who's there?" Her breathless voice chilled in the early morning cold.

"Drop the weapon, Liz…" Aaron's normally smooth-as-caramel Southern drawl held a steely edge to it she'd never heard before. He'd found her. Anticipated her next move.

He stepped closer, the look in his eyes matching his tone. Just for a second she lost what little bit of hope she still clung to. Did he think she was capable of killing Michael?

"Aaron, you scared me." Her voice shook slightly, her nerves wrecked.

"You need to come with me, Liz," he said quietly with regret on his face.

She swallowed back the betrayal she felt at those words. She wouldn't blame Aaron. He was just doing the job he'd been tasked to do.

"I—I can't do that. I didn't kill Michael, but someone wants you to think that I did."

His face twisted with gut-wrenching pain. "I know you didn't kill him, but running makes you look guilty. Come with me. I promise we'll figure it out together. You'll be treated fairly."

She stepped to within inches of him and shook her head sadly. "If you want me to come with you, you'll have to shoot me." She was close enough to witness the battle raging in him as they faced each other in a silent standoff.

"Liz… Don't throw your life away like this."

Aaron's cell phone rang and her already-battered nerves had her jumping at the sound.

He didn't break eye contact as he answered the call. "Yes, Jase." Would he give her up? *Please, God, no.* She had to find a way to convince him to let her go. "Not yet. I'm working a lead now. I'll let you know the minute I have her."

She blew out the breath and leaned over, hands on her knees. He hadn't told Jase. She couldn't imagine how hard that was for Aaron. Jase had been his friend for years.

"I'm sorry, Aaron," she said once he'd ended the call. And she truly was. This wasn't the way she wanted things to go. She turned and headed for the Jeep while silently praying she knew him as well as she thought.

"Liz, stop." With her heart pounding in her

ears, she reached for the door handle and then heard it. *Click, click, click.*

"Run," she yelled, turning from the Jeep. Aaron grabbed her around the waist and all but hauled her away. They'd barely cleared a handful of steps when the Jeep exploded and fire and shrapnel blasted past them like a tidal wave sweeping them in its wake.

Liz hit the ground hard. Landing on her injured wrist, she screamed in agony as searing pain shot through her and she almost blacked out. Seconds later, the cabin nearby exploded and reality struck hard.

Someone had planted a bomb inside the Jeep to be detonated when the door was breeched. The only question was, who was the intended target? Michael or her?

Aaron slowly moved to his knees beside her. He was bleeding from his forehead and his cheek. There were cuts in several spots on his hands.

"Are you okay?" she asked in concern, immediately forgetting her own pain. She couldn't bear it if anything happened to Aaron because of his loyalty to her.

"I'm fine," he dismissed her worry. "How bad is it?" he asked gravely when he saw the way she cradled her injured wrist.

"Not too bad," she lied. She sucked in a sharp breath and closed her eyes as bile rose in her throat and she fought to keep the world around her from spinning out of control.

He clearly wasn't convinced. "Liz, you need to come in with me and have that looked at. We can't stay here. Either that bomb was intended for Michael or someone knew you'd come here and they wanted to eliminate the threat you posed. They don't need you alive to frame you, Liz," he added in a quiet tone. "Let me protect you."

She stumbled to her feet. Cradling her injured wrist close, she put much-needed space between them. "You can't protect me." She swept the devastation with her good hand. "Isn't this obvious? You can't keep me safe. Let me go," she urged passionately. "Please. I'm better off on my own."

He came after her and she backed away, every step taunting her with the realization that alone, she wasn't sure she was up to what lay ahead.

"I won't let them do to you what they did to Michael," he said and she believed he would do everything in his power to fulfill that promise, but at what cost to him?

"Then help me," she pleaded. "I can't stay here any longer. If nothing else, the team will have seen the explosion. It's less than five miles to headquarters. They'll come here to investigate. It'll be over for me."

Liz could see him wavering and she realized how much she needed his help. She quickly told him about the mysterious text message she'd received minutes before she'd found Michael and about the information in the envelope Michael left her. She couldn't bring herself to tell him about her missing weapon just yet.

Aaron shook his head. "It's compelling, but it's not enough to prove you didn't kill Michael. According to Reyna's time of death, Sam was killed first and you were the last person to see Michael alive." The doubt on his face was hard to take.

"Then help me find out who's behind this," she forced the words out. When he didn't answer, she went for broke. "Aaron, you know me. You know I wouldn't do this. I loved Michael like family and no matter what Sam did, I wouldn't take the law into my own hands. It goes against everything I believe." Her voice stumbled for a second.

"Please, I just need time to get to Black Bear and find the evidence Michael left there. That's all I'm asking." She needed Aaron on her side. "Aaron, please. Help me prove my innocence."

Something in the distance dragged her attention from the man standing close to her. She turned in time to see multiple car lights bouncing along the gravel road nearby. Michael's property was the last place on a dead-end road. No one would deliberately come this way without good reason.

Aaron whirled as the approaching vehicles shot through the entrance without regard for the make-shift gate. Right away he knew this was not his people, which left only one explanation. It must be whoever set the explosion.

"We have to get out of here now. Come with me—I have a snowmobile parked just over that ridge." The relief on her face was worth any amount of difficulty he knew they'd face in the future.

Before she could answer, the vehicles opened fire on them.

They ducked low behind a group of trees. "I'll cover you. Get the envelope and head for that ridge over there. I'll catch up with you."

She shook her head stubbornly. "No, I'm not leaving you, Aaron."

"Now, Liz. I've got this."

With one final look his way, she crouched low and hurried for the truck while Aaron shot at the approaching vehicles, forcing them to stop. Several men got out and returned fire.

Out of the corner of his eye, Aaron saw Liz tuck Michael's note with the map to the cabin inside her boot. He'd seen her do that many times in combat. Usually, the enemy didn't think to look inside a person's boot.

Once he was sure Liz was safe, he ducked deep into the woods and zigzagged up to the ridge until he caught up with her. "They'll hear the engine noise, but I know this land like the back of my hand. I've lived here for years." He hopped on the machine and she got on behind him. "Hang on tight. It's pretty rough back here."

Aaron shoved the machine into high gear and took off at a fast speed through the wilderness without any lights. At least the men following them would have to work to find the direction he and Liz had gone.

As they bounced over the rough terrain, he struggled with what to do. He knew Liz hadn't killed Michael—or Sam for that matter—but it appeared someone was trying to set her up to take the fall. If he took her into custody, would he be signing her death certificate? Whoever was behind the murders had proven they could get to whomever they wanted at any time. He couldn't let that happen to Liz. With his head screaming what he needed to do, his heart wouldn't let him. Right or wrong, he wasn't going to let her down.

"I can't keep Jase in the dark for the four days' time it will take to reach Black Bear. Too many things can go wrong in between and we risk the chance of being caught by those men or our people. We'll need a faster way to get there. If we can reach my place, I have a plane I bought and restored a few years back. I keep it at the small airstrip I built on my property."

Truth be told, owning his own plane had been a dream of his for years. Even as a child in Texas, he'd loved the idea of flying. As a teen he'd taken lessons. And when his family moved to Colorado, he'd continued to hone his skills. Then he'd used his flying experience to excel in the military. After he'd left the military, Aaron had become a trainer for special ops. His expertise in flying along with his training skills were some of the reasons why Jase Bradford had initially recruited him for the Scorpions.

Since joining the team, he'd flown just about everything imaginable in all sorts of dangerous situations.

"We can refuel in Talkeetna and then go on to Black Bear once we've spoken to this Rick Evans Michael mentioned in his note." She squeezed his shoulder and her gratitude was worth every risk he knew they'd have to take.

The snowmobile bounced over the snowy landscape strewn with remnants from a recent forest fire. It took all his skills to keep from burying it multiple times while he continuously checked behind them.

The explosion had left him jumpy. So far, they weren't being followed, which he didn't like at all. The men would have reached the destroyed cabin by now. They had to hear the noise of the snowmobile and the direction it was heading. These people were smart. Why weren't they sending people after them?

His hands clutched the handlebars in a tight grip. It seemed like forever before the lights appeared from his makeshift airstrip. He'd smoothed the area out himself. Under normal conditions, there would be no problem taking off or landing, but these weren't normal weather conditions. It had been snowing for a while. Clouds blanketed the mountains from view, and it was still dark out. He dismounted the snowmobile and headed for the hangar. With just the two of them, would he be able to protect her? He didn't dare call in backup; Liz would never make it to Black Bear and her chances of staying free would vanish.

Liz was his friend and he'd seen how violent these men were. They'd gone after Sam in a heavily guarded facility. They'd killed a federal agent. They had nothing to lose. Liz wouldn't stand a chance on her own. He wasn't about to let her fall victim to these monsters.

Like it or not he was all-in, which meant they were on their own.

Something disturbing tore his attention to the edge of the landing strip. Additional vehicles were closing in. Now he understood why the men hadn't followed them. Whoever was behind Michael's and Sam's murders wasn't taking any chances. They'd stationed men where they believed Liz would go for help. Michael's place and his. Which meant they knew about his friendship with Liz. They'd anticipated this move.

"We have to get airborne now if we stand a chance at escaping. I need your help," he yelled over his shoulder.

She didn't hesitate. Once they reached the hangar where the plane was stored, Aaron threw open the doors. Liz helped him unpin the jet and then they got inside. Aaron fired the engine and taxied down the runway.

More than half a dozen vehicles charged the airstrip trying to cut them off. Aaron dodged the two lead vehicles, then swerved hard and managed to keep a somewhat steady path in spite of multiple rounds of gunfire coming their way.

With a silent prayer for their safe assent, Aaron throttled the plane sharply and they were airborne. Once he'd reached a safe height, Aaron veered right, and headed over Painted Rock Mountain while the men below continued firing to try to bring them down.

He grabbed his phone.

"Who are you calling?" Liz asked on edge. It hurt that she thought he'd betray her.

"Jase needs to know what just happened back there." He squeezed her good hand. "Please trust me." She stared at him with those worried eyes before slowly nodding.

Nothing about what happened over the past few weeks made sense. He'd imagined once Sam was in custody, they'd locate the missing weapons and everything would be finished. Yet reality hadn't proven that to be the case.

Time was quickly running out for the investigation to remain with the Scorpion team. If they didn't figure out what was going on soon, Liz would be left to take the fall for everything and they might never find out who was behind the killings or locate the missing weapons.

It took forever for the call to finally go through and once it did the service was so sketchy that he lost it several times.

When he could hear Jase clearly enough, Aaron quickly updated him on what had taken place at Michael's hunting cabin and then again at the landing strip. He didn't mention Liz.

"I know she's with you, Aaron. You need to bring her in for her own safety. This thing is escalating and there's more. We have uncovered some financial records that show a large amount of money was transferred into Liz's bank account recently." The moment he heard those words the bottom fell out of Aaron's stomach. Coupled with what Jase had texted him earlier, things looked bleak.

"I'll get Gavin and some men on the way to your place and Michael's. Whatever else is going on here, bring her in for her own protection, Aaron. And before the stink of this thing lands on you."

Aaron disconnected the call without answering, his thoughts reeling. Jase was smart. It wouldn't take long before he realized Aaron had disobeyed his orders and they'd both gone rogue.

He needed to go dark and soon. Aaron slipped

off the back of his phone and took out the battery. They could trace the phone easily enough when it was on. Taking the battery out would make it more of a challenge. The first opportunity possible, he'd destroy it.

"Where's your phone?" he asked when she stared at him without understanding. "They'll keep coming after us. They'll find a way to track us. We won't have much time."

"It's my burner, Aaron. I left my personal phone at the house. No one on the team has this number," she assured him.

He remembered what she'd said about the text message. "Someone knows it. They texted you the warning."

She squared her shoulders. "We need some way to contact Rick Evans when we get close to Talkeetna. In the note, Michael mentioned he could help us. And how else are we going to reach this Jessie Chena we're to get in touch with in Black Bear?"

He blew out a sigh. She was right. They'd have to risk it. "You're right. But keep it off. We'll only use it as necessary."

She touched his arm. "Thank you, Aaron," she said humbly. "Thank you for believing in me."

He managed a smile...for her. In spite of everything, Liz was a good person. She'd shown that to him time and again. He'd walk through fire to protect her, but he just hoped they could stay alive long enough to figure out who was behind the murders and how the attack tonight was connected to the missing guns.

"What I don't understand is why are they trying to kill me? They've planted enough evidence to make me appear guilty. Wouldn't killing me only shed suspicion on that theory?"

He spared her a searching look. "Not if you're discredited already. And if you're dead, you can't defend yourself." He watched her shiver at the implication.

"These people are cunning, Liz. If they were able to kill a federal agent and get to Sam in a secure prison, once they realize you're still alive and not in prison, they'll be worried you might know something. You're better off dead to them. Hopefully, they don't know about the cabin in Alaska or we're in big trouble." He shook his head and tried to rally his confidence.

They'd been so sure Sam was acting alone. Transporting the weapons to the US for his own diabolical purpose, but what if Sam were just the supplier? How did Michael's death fit into any of this? The note he left Liz seemed to implicate him. The only question was, in what?

He knew Liz was watching him closely and he didn't want to show his doubts. "We'll figure it out," he said with as much conviction as he could muster and then focused his full attention on the task of flying the plane in high-altitude weather conditions while trying to make sense of the last twenty-four hours. Nothing about the murders added up. He had to be missing something key.

"I need you to tell me everything you and Michael discussed and what your last minutes were like with him. I know you said he was acting out of character, but did anything unusual happen?" he asked.

She hesitated and his internal radar went ballistic. Why did she have to think about her answer? *Stop it—this is Liz.*

"Beyond his wanting to speak with Sam in prison, you mean?" She glanced his way.

That certainly had been unexpected, as was the outcome of the visit.

He nodded. "Go on."

"After we left the compound, we went straight to his house..." She stopped as if she'd remembered something. "The car. The one that looked the same as the car last night. It was behind us in his neighborhood. Michael kept watching it. I could tell it made him uneasy, but when I asked if he recognized it, he said no." She turned in her seat to look at him. "Aaron, I'm almost positive it was the same car."

Which seemed to indicate Michael's killer not only knew where he lived but had been keeping tabs on him. Waiting for the moment when he was alone perhaps?

Something she'd said earlier troubled him.

"You mentioned that Michael insisted on talking to Sam, but he never spoke to him. I watched the interview. Michael didn't say a word…" He remembered what happened right before Liz and Michael left the cell.

"He hugged Sam." Aaron glanced her way. "Right before you left, Michael hugged Sam. He whispered something the recorder didn't pick up. What was it?"

She shook her head baffled. "Are you sure? I didn't hear anything."

Regret hit him like a brick wall. He didn't believe her. The video surveillance hadn't lied and she'd been close enough to hear the exchange.

"Aaron, it's true," she said, seeing his doubt. "I admit I was surprised when he hugged Sam. He'd been so angry with him earlier. I just thought it was Michael's way of making peace with the situation."

He recalled what the previous field commander Kyle Jennings had said. He'd had suspicions that someone from the Scorpion team might have been working for Sam's organization. Could it have been Michael? If so, then why were both Michael and Sam dead unless there was someone bigger involved? Perhaps, the intended buyer for the guns. Had Sam and possibly Michael double-crossed that person? If so, it had resulted in a deadly outcome.

With no clear answers in sight, Aaron focused

on another direction. "Michael obviously had access to your passkey. He could have seen where you put it. The only question is who did he give it to and why did they kill him?"

Liz thought about it for a second then shook her head. "I wish I knew…" She hesitated. There was something else she hadn't told him, he could tell.

"Aaron, when I got home after we found Sam…" She stopped for a second. "I'm almost positive someone had been inside my cabin. And there's more." She hesitated and then said, "I keep my spare weapon in my bedroom closet. It's missing. Someone took it."

Shocked, he stared at her in disbelief. He knew she kept a Glock. Would it turn out to be Michael's murder weapon? Coupled with what Jase had uncovered about Liz's past, he was certain she was being set up to take the blame for everything.

"Liz, after what happened with the missing weapons in Pennsylvania and the accusations made by Sam's second-in-command about one of our team being dirty, we've been digging into the personnel files of everyone. You're the only one who has a connection with Sam from the past. You went to the same university for crying out loud, and then you end up attending the CIA training facility around the same time? That's an awfully big coincidence and to anyone else looking on, it appears the two of you have known each other for a while. It speaks of a possible connection to a terrorist."

Her face fell. "I told you Sam and I were friends. I was honest about that."

She was right. Liz had told him that she and Sam had hung out a lot while Sam's team was working in the same area as the Scorpions and that they'd become friends. Which was Liz's nature. She rarely met a person she didn't befriend.

"Yes, but you didn't tell me about attending the same university or that you were at the CIA training facility around the same time." He paused for a second to take in her startled reaction.

"That's because I didn't know about them. Aaron, I never knew Sam when I was in college and the training facility is big. You know that."

"There's more, Liz." He told her about the large amount of money that had been transferred into her account.

There was no way she could fake that much astonishment. In his mind there was no doubt. Liz wouldn't betray her team or her country in such a way, but proving her innocence against the increasing evidence that said otherwise was going to be a near-impossible task.

THREE

Something jarred her awake. Caught between sleep and consciousness, her heart in her throat, Liz jerked toward Aaron. He held the controls of the plane in a vise grip, struggling with all his strength to keep it in the air.

Outside, what looked like blizzard conditions made it next to impossible to see more than a few inches in front of them as an onslaught of icy pellets blasted the plane.

Liz fought back a scream as the increasing turbulence sent the plane dipping in the air some fifty feet.

"What's happening?" she shouted above the noise. Aaron was white as a sheet. He was fighting so hard for her.

He spared her a glance. "The weather's been deteriorating for a while now. We're approaching all-out whiteout conditions. We need to find someplace to land and fast, before the storm does it for us." He fought to bring the plane under control.

"We can't go much farther like this." The grimness in his voice hammered home the severity of their situation.

The fine lines around Aaron's eyes had deepened. He looked beyond exhausted and her heart swelled with gratitude. He was doing everything to help her. Risking both his life and his career. She owed him her life. How did you repay such a debt?

"Where are we?" she asked.

"Over Canadian airspace still…I think. I've lost power to some of my instruments. I'm guessing we're about forty-five minutes outside of Talkeetna." He hesitated and then said, "I'm going to see if I can raise this Rick fellow on the radio. I just hope we're close enough."

Aaron grabbed the mic. "Mayday, Mayday, Mayday. This is a distress call for Rick Evans. Come in, Rick." Static was his only answer and he shook his head, frustrated.

"I can't afford to give out my call numbers. We can't identify ourselves because we don't know who might be listening." After another failed attempt Aaron said, "The weather's not helping and we're probably too far away for him to be able to pick us up under these conditions."

In Liz's mind there was only one option. "I'll try texting him. It's worth a shot and maybe the message will go through." She took out her phone, but he grabbed her arm, stopping her.

"What if we're wrong about this guy? We don't know if we can trust him, Liz. He could be working for the people who killed Michael and Sam."

He was right, but there wasn't any other way. "We're all out of options. We don't have a choice."

After a second's hesitation, he slowly nodded. "Do it."

Liz took the note from her boot and typed in the number Michael had provided in his note and kept the message brief. She explained that Michael had told her to get in touch when they were close and that they would be landing under emergency conditions. As soon as the message went through, she replaced the note.

The plane lurched sideways then dipped downward. Liz prayed for their safety while Aaron fought with everything he had to keep the plane from continuing its downward spiral. The weather was worsening by the minute. She'd barely gotten to *amen* when the phone's message alert sounded, startling her. She quickly read the message aloud. "It's Rick. He sent the coordinates. God is good." She smiled in amazement.

"Yes, He is. Let Rick know we're less than half an hour away."

She sent the message and the response was quick. "He'll be waiting for us at the airstrip." She swallowed back her fears. "I just hope we're not making the worst mistake of our lives by trusting him." Her sleep-deprived brain struggled to remember Michael mentioning him before. She was almost positive he hadn't. What did that mean?

"Me too, but like you said, he's all we've got right now. Maybe he can shed some light on what was going on with Michael." He glanced her way. "And I didn't want to mention this before, but we're not exactly legal here. We've been flying without permission the whole way. Let's just hope we've gone undetected by the authorities as well as the killer."

Liz shivered because she understood what that meant. If caught they'd be in serious trouble and could face charges. Another something to be sorry for. Aaron was compromising his principles as well as his life to save hers.

Aaron squinted out the side window searching for the airstrip. "There! I see the lights of the landing strip," he said and breathed out a heavy sigh. "Thank You." He lifted his eyes toward heaven with heartfelt gratitude.

As he began his descent, crosswinds fought the plane every inch of the way, shifting it sideways. The plane shook so hard that Liz worried it would disintegrate around them. Gusts of air caught the wings, forcing the plane off course. It took three tries just to get low enough to make an attempt at a successful landing.

Aaron white-knuckled the plane at a sideways angle, called crabbing, on its final descent.

Once the plane finally came to a jarring halt,

Aaron let out a long breath and Liz closed her eyes briefly and tried to slow her accelerated heart rate.

When she looked at him once more, she could see the extent of what he'd gone through written on his pale face. She hoped the rest of the trip wouldn't be as harrowing as this part had been.

"I've flown through dangerous situations in my time, but that had to be the hairiest. Are you okay?" he asked.

She managed a nod and their eyes met: the gentleness she saw in him left her feeling a little off-balanced. "Yes, I think so."

"Let's hope that's the worst thing we see today," he said to lighten the moment.

She smiled genuinely. He'd fought so hard and she owed him her life. "Let's hope." As they continued to watch each other, something shifted in his eyes and suddenly it was painful to breathe. For the first time she was seeing a different side of the man she'd been proud to call a friend and to serve beside.

Strong and rugged, she realized something she hadn't considered before. Aaron was a handsome man. She hadn't thought about anyone else like that since Eric. He'd been the love of her life, even though they'd been married only a short five years when he'd gone on that final mission for the CIA and it had claimed his life.

A noise of an approaching vehicle broke the

spell between them. Aaron looked away embarrassed and she could finally catch her breath.

"That must be Evans," he said without looking at her. She tried to regroup. They were going into this thing blind without any idea who this man was other than someone Michael trusted, which wasn't exactly comforting. From all indications, Michael may have been working for Sam.

Aaron grabbed his weapon from where he'd stowed it and tucked it behind his back. "Keep yours close," he said and she didn't miss the taut set of his jaw. Liz quickly slipped the Glock inside her jacket pocket.

"Ready?" he asked holding her gaze once more.

She quickly assured him with a nod. "Let's get out of here," he said and grabbed her backpack. She could feel Michael's note from where it lay hidden inside her boot for safekeeping.

Outside the plane's shelter, a biting cold wind ripped through her jacket instantly chilling her to the bone and she hugged the garment closer.

"Where is he?" she asked as she glanced around the remote areas. In the distance, she spotted a cluster of lights low to the ground.

"Are those the lights of Talkeetna?" she asked as Aaron followed her line of sight.

The terse shake of his head assured her that the coiled nerves in the pit of her stomach were justified.

"That's not Talkeetna. Its twenty miles east of

here. From the way the lights are moving I'd say those are snowmobiles." She could see he was concerned and her uneasiness doubled. "We need to get out of the open. We're out in the middle of nowhere with no means to escape should we be attacked."

She understood. She felt exposed as well. "I don't see Rick anywhere. Were we wrong to trust him?" she asked uneasily.

"I don't know, but if he doesn't get here soon, we could be in trouble," Aaron said while keeping a close eye on the snowmobile lights.

"Hello there," someone called out, startling them both and they turned. Aaron with his weapon ready to use.

"Whoa." A man of medium build, dressed in a heavy parka stood next to the row of hangars. "I'm Rick Evans. You two the ones who phoned for help?"

The whiteout conditions had prevented them from seeing the man standing next to a Sno-Cat. The vehicle was truck-sized, had an enclosed cab, and was fully tracked and designed for moving on heavily snowed areas. In this part of the country, such a vehicle would be imperative for getting about in these conditions. "Yes, we are," Aaron said and lowered his gun.

The man headed their way. When he was close, he stuck out his hand. "I'm Rick Evans. You must be Michael's friend," he said to Liz.

Exhaustion seeped through her limbs. It took her a second to realize Michael must have told this man about her.

She took his hand. "That's right. Liz Ramirez." She turned to Aaron. "This is Aaron Foster."

"I hate to cut this short but we have a more immediate problem," Aaron said after he'd shaken Rick's hand. He pointed to the lights. "Any idea who your neighbors are?"

Rick whirled around. "No clue. There are no neighbors around here. My place is the only house this side of Talkeetna. Mostly the airstrip is used for people who come here to trap up in the high country." He shook his head. "I know most of the owners of the hangars and as far as I know, none of them are in the area right now."

Liz fought her gut instinct to ask more questions first. Michael might have trusted this man, but she didn't. Unfortunately, there was no other choice. She and Aaron were freezing and at a disadvantage. They didn't know the lay of the land.

Even after they were safely inside the cab of the Sno-Cat and leaving the airstrip, her uneasiness just wouldn't go away.

"They're probably trappers," Rick assured her after correctly interpreting her concern. "They could be expecting a supply delivery today or waiting to be picked up. This airstrip is used as a drop off spot for the pilots who fly the trappers out around this time of year."

On the surface, Rick's explanation was plausible, but she could see Aaron didn't buy it either. As much as she wanted to think those men being here was little more than a coincidence, with what had just happened back at Michael's hunting cabin in Colorado, they couldn't afford to be wrong about it. Because both of their lives now depended on it.

"My place is only another couple of miles. Unfortunately, we'll be traveling over some really nasty country," Rick said in way of an apology. "That's the main reason why I brought the Sno-Cat. It takes the snowy terrain like it's a walk in the park. Unlike a snowmobile."

While the man seemed genuinely sincere, Aaron couldn't let go of his misgivings. Why didn't Rick seem more concerned about the approaching vehicles?

Aaron sat back in his seat and watched as the Cat ate up the territory in front of them. After managing to land the plane in some of the worst conditions he'd ever flown in, his nerves were still on edge.

"How did you and Michael meet?" Aaron asked because he wanted to make sure Rick's story matched up with what Michael had said in his note.

Rick spared him a friendly glance. "We met a few years back when I flew him to Black Bear for the first time. It's a four-hour flight there, so we got to know it each pretty well. How's he doing, by the way?"

Aaron could almost feel Liz warning him not to say too much. Rick appeared not to know Michael was dead. Was it all an act?

"He's okay." He hated the necessity of the lie yet Rick didn't seem to notice anything out of the ordinary. Had he really gotten that good at deceiving people? The thought didn't sit well.

"Are you two here for the trapping or something else?" Rick kept his eyes on the path ahead. While the question appeared harmless enough, under the current conditions, Aaron found himself second-guessing everything.

"We were on our way to Black Bear when the storm hit. Michael told us about your operation so we decided to see if we could wait the storm out here. Sorry to have to drag you out in such weather, but we're very grateful you were around. With the weather getting worse, we wouldn't have made it much farther."

Rick nodded without looking his way. "No problem. I'm just glad I hadn't left already. I was getting ready to pack up and leave in a few days to go back home to Vancouver."

"So you don't live here full-time?" Aaron asked in surprise. He'd just assumed the man was full-time.

"Oh, no. I live in Vancouver with my wife and

kids. I came here...to wait on a client who apparently isn't coming."

Was it just his imagination or did Rick hesitate ever so slightly. It was enough to raise the hackles on the back of his neck. "That's too bad," Aaron muttered in attempt to cover his unease.

"It happens." Rick admitted with a lift of his shoulders. "In my line of work, you're doing good if one out of every three or four calls ends up in actual work."

Aaron glanced sideways at Liz. She looked beyond tired. Physically, she was running on empty, emotionally she had to be beyond drained. She needed rest.

"How's the wrist?" he asked her quietly. He was worried about her with good reason. The bitter cold they were dealing with made everything more difficult.

"It's okay," she whispered in a thready voice. He could tell nothing was further from the truth. She was pale and drawn. As much as neither of them wanted to admit it, should those men come after them, she'd be at a disadvantage.

In spite of Rick's explanation, something about those snowmobiles didn't add up.

"So Rick, how'd they get the snowmobiles out here in the middle of nowhere?"

That Rick took his time answering did ease Aaron's mind a little bit.

"They probably stored them in one of the hangars. I'm sure there are lots of people who come up here that I've never heard of before."

Aaron kept quiet because what Rick said now seemed to contradict his earlier claims of knowing everyone.

"People fly in and out of the area without letting anyone know about it all the time. It's not uncommon," Rick added as he maneuvered the Cat through a particularly narrow stretch of deep snow where trees kept the area shaded. It seemed Rick had a plausible answer for everything.

The man cast Aaron a curious glance. "You mind telling me what this is all about, Aaron? Are you working for the CIA like Michael was?"

Like Michael *was*…those were the only words that registered beyond the fact that Rick knew Michael was CIA.

He glanced at Liz. She'd caught the slipup too. Was it just an accident that Rick had referred to Michael's employer in past tense?

That Michael had divulged working for the CIA to this man meant he must have trusted him. The only question was why? Because he knew he'd have his back, or because Rick worked for Sam too?

"Michael told you he was CIA?" he answered Rick's question with one of his own and Rick smiled.

"He did. As I said, it's a long flight to Black Bear and usually when Michael came out, he spent the night here before we flew out early the following morning. At first, I thought he was some crackpot claiming to be something he wasn't to impress people, but the more I got to know Michael, I realized he was the real deal. He never told me what he did for the CIA, only that he worked for them."

Rick cleared the woods and the headlights of the Sno-Cat swept over a tiny cabin.

"This is it. It isn't much, but it's warm and dry, and I built it myself," Rick said with obvious pride. "I used to help my old man build houses before I joined the Marines. This one was kind of my tribute to him."

Rick hopped out and headed up the steps of the cabin while Aaron and Liz lagged behind.

"What do you make of him?" she whispered and he drew her close so that only she could hear his answer.

"Frankly, I don't trust him. He's a little too obliging for my taste and he has a plausible answer for everything. Come on, we'd better get inside before he gets suspicious," he whispered against her hair then took her good hand and together they went inside.

A woodstove loaded with fuel burned aggressively in one corner of the living room, heating the entire cabin.

"Come inside. Make yourself at home. The

kitchen's small, but plenty of room for a couple of people. There's a bedroom and bath down the hall."

"Thanks for taking us in, Rick. We're very grateful," Aaron told him while Liz went over to the fire to warm herself. "Does your family get to come here with you very often?"

"Sometimes," Rick told them. "Just not as often as they'd like. They love it here, but mostly this place is my office, so to speak."

His answer didn't really do much to shed any light on Rick's life, Aaron thought.

"Well, you've been more than gracious and I don't know how we can ever repay you." Liz smiled gratefully and Rick beamed.

"No need for that. You're very welcome. I'm happy to help and just glad I was here."

Aaron surveyed the small cabin. There were very few personal items around the place, which backed up Rick's story that it was mostly used for business. Still, if he spent much time here wouldn't he want some reminders of the family he was separated from?

"As much as we'd like to hang out a while, as soon as the weather lifts we have to be on our way. We don't have much time."

Rick stared out the window at the semidarkness as the storm intensified. "It could be a few hours still. These types of fronts blow through here a lot. I've been listening to the weather report and this one's got the makings of a bugger. Can I offer you two something to eat while you wait? I was about to make some breakfast for myself when you texted. You look like you could use something warm inside you."

Aaron tried to remember the last time he'd eaten anything. Probably at lunchtime the day before. It felt like longer. He still couldn't believe two people were dead and he and Liz were racing across the country as fugitives to try and clear her name on the promise of a man whose recent activity was shady at best.

"Actually, that sounds wonderful," Liz said in appreciation.

They had a long way to go still and she was injured. She'd need to rebuild her strength.

"Well, okay, then. How does bacon and eggs sound?" Rick asked with a smile creasing his face.

"It sounds great, but let us help you out." She headed for the kitchen when Rick all but shooed her out.

"No...I've got this," he added quickly. "You guys look bushed. Take a load off for a while."

Liz shook her head and went back to the living room and she and Aaron sat down together.

"Do you think he's working for the people who killed Michael and Sam?" she whispered, while keeping her eyes on the storm raging just beyond the shelter of the cabin.

"I'm not sure. I can't get a good read off him. He acts as if he doesn't know about Michael's death, but it could be just that. Until we're sure, I don't trust him."

She nodded. "That's my thought too. What about the men on the snowmobiles? It seems like an odd coincidence that they'd be out here at the same time as Rick and right as we arrived."

"Yes, but still, I can't believe they found out where we were going so quickly. On the other hand, they could have known about Alaska already. Michael might have told them, even." She froze at the suggestion that they might be heading into a setup.

Liz shifted in her seat inches away. The sincerity in her eyes tore at his heart. It made him want to fight with everything he could muster to save her. Clear her name. And his very reaction scared him.

He hadn't felt this way about a woman since Beth's betrayal. Even today, it still had the power to turn his stomach. He'd gone against his better judgment in falling in love with a subordinate. He'd trusted Beth with everything and she'd ripped his heart to shreds, blaming him for her mistakes that had led to a failed extraction attempt and multiple lives lost.

"I'm so sorry about this, Aaron," Liz murmured.

He slowly let the past go back where it belonged. "You've nothing to be sorry for," he said fervently. "None of this is your fault."

She slowly nodded. "Maybe, but I hate that I've dragged you into my troubles. I've put you and Jase at odds and… Aaron, you could lose your job over this…or worse."

He captured her good hand in his. "We'll get through this. Whatever this is about, we'll figure it out together. You're not alone anymore."

Liz inched closer, her eyes dark with unspoken emotions that he'd give anything to explore. He leaned in just a smidgen, smoothing away the worry lines from around her eyes with his fingers. His gaze slipped over her pretty face. He hated that this was happening to her.

"Breakfast is ready," Rick said without looking at them. Aaron got to his feet and held out his hand to her.

She stared up at him for the longest time before she took his hand and together they went to the dining room. "Something smells good," Aaron said with a catch in his throat.

"It's not much to brag on, but its protein and it'll give you some energy. I have a feeling you two are going to need all the help you can get." Rick motioned to a couple of chairs on the opposite side of the table. "Have a seat."

Aaron pulled one of the chairs out for Liz and she smiled up at him. One of the things Aaron and Liz shared was their faith. Facing death and a whole lot of long nights, they'd had plenty of time to talk about what their lives had been like before the Scorpions. While he hadn't been able to talk about Beth, it had been a surprise to learn that he'd once worked with her late husband. Eric was a good man. It was easy to see she'd loved him deeply. After more than five years, Liz still mourned his passing.

"Do you mind if I offer a prayer, Rick?" Aaron asked and the man shook his head without speaking.

Aaron bowed his head. "Father, we are so grateful for Your safe passage here and we ask Your blessing on the rest of the trip and we thank You for Rick's assistance today. Amen."

"Amen," Liz murmured, but Rick didn't look at them. Aaron sensed he'd been embarrassed at being included in the prayer.

"Eat it while it's hot," Rick muttered and took a forkful of eggs.

Aaron dug into his food with enthusiasm. A simple spread of eggs and bacon tasted like a five-star meal in his book.

"I can't remember when food has been this good before," Aaron said with a thankful smile.

Liz laughed. "I know. I've had some wonderful meals all over the world, but this one right here tops the list. And this coffee is delicious."

Aaron noticed something then that sent up all sorts of alarms. Rick kept glancing out the window. Was he simply checking the weather or expecting someone?

"Everything okay there, Rick?" he asked and the man's attention jerked to him.

"What? Oh, sure, sure. I'm just worried about the storm. It...doesn't appear to be easing any and I know you two are eager to be on your way." Rick's jaw clenched over the obvious lie.

Before Aaron could muster an answer, a noise outside dragged his attention from the conversation. Engines closing in. Aaron leaped to his feet and headed for the window while killing the lights. Liz and Rick followed on his heels.

It was still semidark out and easy to see the headlights of multiple vehicles heading their way.

"Are you expecting company?" Aaron asked and rounded on Rick warily. The man had definitely grown nervous and he couldn't look Aaron in the eye.

Rick shook his head. "They're not here for me. You two go in the back and I'll see if I can get rid of them. If something goes south, I keep a snowmobile in a shed just over the next hilltop behind the house. If you can get to it, go back to the airstrip. My Challenger is in the hangar next to yours. It's fueled and ready. It's better equipped to handle a storm like this."

Aaron hesitated. Something felt off. But the snowmobiles were almost right on top of them and they had no idea who those men were.

Rick waited by the door while Liz rushed to the table and took their plates to the kitchen and out of sight, then she and Aaron went to the bedroom and closed the door without turning on any lights.

Headlights flashed across the window near the bed and they both ducked. Outside Aaron heard men talking and he crept over to the window.

"They're stopping. It looks like they're searching behind the cabin," he said in a hushed voice. "I count at least three snowmobiles. There's more around front. I don't like it, Liz. It feels like a setup."

She stood next to him. "It does. I just don't understand how they found us so quickly."

"We don't know who these guys are yet. They might just be trappers who were curious about our arrival. I'm sure having a plane fly in here isn't exactly a daily occurrence."

He could see that she didn't believe him. "Aaron, we have to get to the cabin in Black Bear. If we don't, we may never know who killed Michael and Sam, or where the missing weapons have gone."

Although she didn't say as much, he knew it was on her mind. Without the evidence, they might never clear her name.

"We'll make it there," he insisted. "I promise we will. There's no way I'm going to let you go to jail for what someone else did."

Liz put her hand to her head and swayed.

His arms circled her waist for support. "Are you okay?" he asked with growing concern.

She shook her head. "No, something's wrong, Aaron. I feel so..." She barely got the words out when her eyes rolled back in her head and she went limp in his arms.

He felt for a pulse. It was there, but weak. What if the injuries from the crash had been worse than the doctor believed? She might have internal bleeding or who knows what else.

Aaron forgot everything except the woman in his arms. He couldn't let anything happen to her. He picked her up and headed for the nearby bed when the world around him began to spin uncontrollably and his vision blurred. He stumbled several times, then lost his footing. He was losing consciousness. He dropped to his knees with Liz still in his arms.

It was a struggle to stay alert. He became aware of a door closing and men talking quietly. Someone was in the house. Was Rick in danger?

"Did you take care of them?" someone asked. A man. He sounded so far away. The world around Aaron grew fuzzy and he fought the darkness.

"Yes, they're here. It will take a few minutes for the drug to take effect." Rick's voice was as clear as the realization that he'd put something in their food.

Aaron's eyelids felt as if they were weighted down with lead. He was barely hanging on. Sam had been poisoned. Was the same thing happening to them? Had Michael already given up the location for the guns and he and Liz had now become expendable?

Numbness swept through his body quickly. Aaron's last conscious thought was that the man Michael had trusted Liz's life to had betrayed both of them in the worst possible way.

FOUR

Through the fog of disorientation surrounding her, voices could be heard. They were close. Liz struggled to open her eyes, but it was as if they were glued shut. Her head pounded as if someone had struck her hard. With her fuzzy thoughts, she tried to make sense of what had happened. The last thing she remembered was hiding with Aaron at the back of the cabin. Then the dizziness set in…

Rick. Through her muddled thoughts one thing became obvious. He'd set them up. The kindness he'd shown them had all been an act. She and Aaron had been drugged by someone Michael trusted. They'd been right to have doubts about Rick, but it was of little consolation now.

She sensed movement nearby and tensed.

"Get her awake. Now." An angry voice issued the command. "We need answers. We've waited long enough for the weapons."

For the weapons.

She was slapped with so much force that her head twisted in the opposite direction. Pain shot down the side of her face bringing stinging tears. For a second, she thought she might lose consciousness again.

Aaron! Where was he? Fear surged through her like an electrical current. She struggled to hang on. Force her eyes open. Her arms and legs were immobile.

When the world finally focused, she realized she was being restrained on one of the kitchen chairs. Hands tied behind her back, causing her injured limb to throb mercilessly.

She glanced around frantically searching for Aaron. He was seated next to her. Ropes restrained his chest. His hands were secured behind his back, his legs tied like hers. He didn't move and her heart dropped to her feet. Was he alive?

Please, God.

Through slitted eyes, she counted half a dozen men standing around. None of which she recognized. Rick stood off to himself, leaning against the door.

The men would have found their Glocks and taken them. They were both restrained and defenseless. She moved her foot slightly. The note was still there. They hadn't searched her boot.

"She's awake," the man standing over her said to someone else.

Liz forced Rick into eye contact. "How could you do this? Michael trusted you."

He shook his head and looked away without answering.

A swarthy man with cold eyes stepped into her line of sight, blocking out everything else. "Shut up. You are in no position to ask questions." His face contorted with the anger that was reflected in his voice. He was close enough for her to see every line and every pore on his ruddy face. His foul breath was repulsive.

Without breaking eye contact he barked in her face to someone, "Take Evans with you. Search the plane. Let me know what you find." To Liz he seethed, "You'd better hope for both your sakes that we find them. Otherwise…"

The man was clearly in charge. He stepped away and Liz realized they were looking for the missing weapons.

One of the armed men grabbed Rick and forced him out of the cabin. The very act seemed to indicate Rick wasn't part of their organization, but had somehow been forced into cooperation.

The man in charge followed them outside. Liz's eyes darted to Aaron and she saw that he was awake.

"It won't take them long to figure out the weapons aren't there," he whispered so that only she could hear.

She knew exactly what he meant. They didn't

have much time. "We're outmanned. Including the leader, I counted six men other than Rick. There could be more outside. We have to find a way to divide and conquer, otherwise once they realize we don't know where the guns are, they'll kill us."

Aaron started to say something, but one of the remaining men turned and stared at them. "Keep quiet," he snapped, then turned back to his friend.

"Just follow my lead, okay?" Aaron mouthed.

Before she could respond, the leader came back inside and immediately headed for Liz.

She could see the rage on his face. "I'm done playing nice. If you want to save yourself, tell us where you hid the weapons." He moved to within inches of her and grabbed her hair, pulling her closer. "Where are they?" he snarled.

She had little doubt these men were part of the crew who had been double-crossed by Sam. They'd been expecting a delivery that didn't happen. And they somehow believed Liz knew where the weapons were hidden.

"I don't know what you're talking about," she managed and closed her eyes, her thoughts reeling.

How had they tied Rick to Michael? She'd checked Michael's phone. There were no calls made recently. Unless... Michael's burner phone. It was missing. What if the person who killed him had taken it? Was that how Michael arranged for the guns to be moved?

The man's facial expression contorted in rage. "You're lying. Michael Harris was your partner. You knew exactly what was going on. You were on Lansford's payroll."

Liz's shocked gaze locked on the man. He believed she was on Sam's payroll. Had Michael told him as much or had Sam lied to try and spare his own life?

The man smiled knowingly. "That's right. *He* told me that you worked for Lansford just like your dirty partner."

He…who was he talking about? Unease slithered up her spine. Was this goon just the muscle for someone else? Someone far bigger?

"I don't work for Lansford and I have no idea what you're talking about." She threw the words in his face. The man snorted. Before he could say more, one of the others came over and whispered something in his ear.

The leader stared at her, then drew his hand back and slapped Liz hard once more. The impact had her seeing stars, her head flying sideways. The throbbing pain intensified.

The man lifted his hand to strike her again, but Aaron stopped him. "That's enough," he said as he fought against his restraints. The look in his eyes was murderous. Liz had no doubt he would have killed the man if he could have gotten loose.

"Shut up," the leader snapped at Aaron and then glared at Liz. "Enough games. The weapons aren't on the aircraft and they were not at the location they were supposed to be in Black Bear." He paused for her to get the full effect of his glare. "I want the truth. Now," he roared loud enough so that she jumped.

He'd let slip that the guns were supposed to be in Black Bear.

Out of the corner of her eye she saw Aaron's shocked reaction. He'd caught it too. The men had been to Black Bear already. Had they found the evidence?

She struggled to keep from losing hope. Somehow, she had to find a way to convince the man that she knew nothing about Sam's operation.

"I'm telling you the truth," she said with as much passion as she could muster. "I don't know anything about the guns and I'm certainly not part of any criminal activity."

The man was unmoved. She tried a different tactic. "You've just kidnapped two federal agents. I'd say you have more to worry about than finding some weapons."

His expression didn't waver. He knew who they were and he wasn't worried about being prosecuted for the kidnapping, which told her it didn't matter whether or not they cooperated. She and Aaron wouldn't be leaving this cabin alive. The urgency of their situation just ratcheted to desperate.

After seconds of a silent standoff, he stepped away.

"I need to speak with the boss. Find out what he wants me to do with these." He informed one of his minions and then he stepped outside and out of their hearing.

"Did you hear what he said?" she whispered to Aaron in astonishment.

He briefly nodded. "If he's not the one in charge, then who is?"

She quickly glanced at the door. "Exactly, and how is Rick involved in this thing?"

In Aaron's eyes she saw the same questions rattling round in her head. "I don't think Rick's working for them by choice. Not that that's any consolation," he said.

"They've been to Black Bear. What if they found the evidence?" she voiced her worst fear.

Aaron's gaze softened and he tried to reassure her. "Don't go there, Liz. We don't know that they have any clue about the cabin or the evidence."

She was struggling not to give up. Looking into his eyes, she saw the strength she needed.

Outside, angry voices engaged in a heated argument. One was the leader. She couldn't make out the exchange but it was obvious that the leader wasn't happy.

"Aaron, if we don't produce a location for the guns, they'll kill us."

He glanced at the door and then back to her. "I have an idea that might buy us some time. Do you think you can manage to get your hands free? I noticed that the knot isn't too tight."

She tested the ropes ignoring the excruciating pain that shot up her arm from her injured wrist. "Yes, I'm pretty sure I can work the ropes loose…" Before she finished the leader returned and she stopped what she was doing.

It was clear the minute she saw his face that the conversation with the person in charge hadn't gone well.

The man stormed up in front of Liz. "You will tell me the location now or you will suffer the consequences. You've wasted enough time."

She stared up at his fury. Fear for their lives had now doubled.

When she didn't respond, he turned his attention to Aaron. "Perhaps torturing *him* will get you to talk," he said with deadly intent.

Please, no. She struggled against her restraints and the man laughed.

Aaron's gaze locked with hers. So many unspoken emotions flashed in his eyes. She understood all of them, because she felt the same. She cared about Aaron deeply. She didn't want to die like this. In the middle of nowhere, at the hands of thugs, being held for something they had no control over.

"I'm okay," he assured her.

Liz forced herself to breathe normally. She glanced around at the men. All were heavily armed. They were spaced around the living and kitchen area. Restrained, she and Aaron were powerless.

She felt around until she was able to access the knot used to tie her hands. The pain in her injured wrist made even the slightest of movements feel as if someone were stabbing her with hot knives. Yet there was no other choice. If she could ignore the ache and get her restraints loose, she'd have a matter of seconds to free Aaron and subdue the men. It seemed an impossible situation.

Fighting through the nausea, she began working the restraints. She had to go slow, keeping her movement to a minimum so as not to draw attention to herself.

The leader took out his knife and held it against Aaron's throat. He turned to her once more. "Well? Do I kill him or will you talk?"

At the introduction of the knife, her heart thundered against her chest. "Let him go. He's not part of this."

Aaron's gaze sliced to hers. "No, Liz. It's time to tell them the truth."

She stared at him trying to interpret the meaning behind those words. She trusted him completely. She'd let whatever he had planned play out.

"They want the weapons. We want to live." She slowly nodded.

The leader obviously had his doubts, but the renewed anger in him indicated whoever he'd called hadn't been happy with his results so far. If that person was the one responsible for Michael and Sam's deaths, then they wouldn't think twice about killing this man if he didn't produce results.

With narrowed eyes, he stared first at Aaron and then at Liz before loosening the knife slightly.

"That's more like it. Cooperate and maybe we'll let you walk away. But you'd better not be playing me, or else it will be my pleasure to kill both of you in the most painful way possible."

Liz did her best to sound convincing. "Aaron, you can't tell them."

"I told you to shut up!" the man growled before turning to Aaron. "Where are they?"

Aaron didn't hesitate. "They're not here, but I know where they're hidden. I can fly you there."

The man snorted his doubt. "You're lying. You'd say anything to save yourself."

Aaron's expression never altered. "Am I? You want your guns, don't you? Then untie me and I'll take you to them."

The man didn't break eye contact. After several seconds of silence, he seemed to waver. "All right, we'll see if you're telling the truth. You'll take us to them, but she stays here." He pointed the knife at Liz.

"That's not part of the deal," Aaron argued. "If you want the guns we both go."

The man whipped the knife out and held it against Liz's throat. "You're not in a position to give orders. She stays behind or else she dies. Your choice."

"All right," Aaron interjected quickly. "I'll do what you say. She stays behind. Just don't hurt her."

The leader jeered then slowly lowered the knife. "I thought you'd like that option better."

Aaron smiled reassuringly at her. The tenderness on his face tore at her heart.

"It'll be okay. Just keep doing what you're doing. Before you know it we'll be free and together and we'll fly out of here once more."

She understood. He was trying to draw the leader and hopefully some of his team away so that they could divide and conquer. It would give her time to escape. She had to free herself and disarm the men left behind as quickly as possible. Then she needed to reach the airstrip before Aaron got in the air, because once they discovered he was bluffing, they wouldn't hesitate to kill him.

The leader motioned to one of his men. "Untie

him and bring him with us." Then he turned his full attention to Aaron. "I'm warning you, this had better not be a trick, otherwise, I'll notify my men. She'll be dead."

"I understand," Aaron said calmly.

Once he was free, the leader grabbed Aaron's arm, yanked him to his feet and then jerked him toward the door. "You come with me," he ordered two of his men. "The rest of you keep an eye on her. If she tries anything...kill her."

Just before he was forced from the cabin Aaron glanced her way. Emotions she couldn't begin to explain had her drawing in a deep breath.

"Be careful," she mouthed and then he was gone and it was all up to her now.

"Hurry up," the leader yelled and then shoved Aaron toward one of the snowmobiles parked out front. "Your friend back there wasted enough of our time already. She should have done what was expected of her."

What was expected of her? The words played through Aaron's head uneasily. Was it another ploy to try and convince him of Liz's guilt or was there something more at play here?

"What are you talking about?" Aaron asked on a long shot.

The man seemed to have second thoughts about speaking out of turn. "Nothing. Get on the machine. You're driving. I'm warning you, you'd better not try anything…" Before he could finish the insult, the man's phone rang and he grabbed it out of his pocket. Once he saw who the caller was, he motioned to one of his goons.

"Watch the prisoner. It's him." The man grabbed Aaron's arm while the leader moved away.

"Yes, sir," The leader said into the phone with an entirely humble disposition. "No, not yet, but he claims to know where Lansford and Harris moved them." When he shot him a look, Aaron tried not to let on that he'd been listening to the conversation.

"Our people have searched the plane, the weapons aren't here, but he says they're at a different location." After a lengthy silence where Aaron believed the guy in charge showed his displeasure, the man answered. "Don't worry—if it's a lie, they'll both regret it. It will be my pleasure to kill them."

The man ended the call and shoved the phone in his pocket. He came back to Aaron. "You'd better be telling the truth," he said and pushed Aaron toward the machine once more.

"Follow them," he ordered once they were both on. Aaron fired up the machine and steered it behind one of the men.

"Where did you and Ramirez hide the weapons?" the leader said with obvious agitation, no doubt suspecting Aaron was shining him on.

Aaron chose his words carefully. "How do I know you won't kill me and Liz once you have them?"

"You don't," he man said smugly. "Why do I get the feeling you're stringing me along? All it takes is one call...and she's dead."

Dread spread through his body like a disease. Aaron realized he had to do something and quickly, otherwise, he and Liz were goners.

Thinking quickly, he revved the machine into high gear and rammed into the back of the snowmobile in front of them. The other driver jerked the controls and swerved several times trying to keep the machine on the trail, but he wasn't skilled enough to pull it off. The snowmobile took off across the woods and buried itself nose first in a deep snowdrift.

Both men jumped off. Aaron realized it was now or never.

Before he had a chance to disarm the leader, the man realized what he intended to do and shoved the knife against Aaron's throat. "I don't think so. Stop the machine. Now," he ordered.

Aaron grabbed for the knife. The two struggled back and forth. Aaron finally managed to get the knife from the man. He slowed the machine to a halt, then dragged the leader off and in front of him. He shoved the knife against the leader's throat as one of the other men charged for them. The man stopped when he spotted the knife.

"Get him," the leader yelled. Aaron noticed the man was alone. Where was the second person? Aaron pushed the leader hard and he stumbled to the ground. Turning back to the snowmobile, Aaron climbed on. Before he could put the machine in gear, someone shoved the barrel of an assault rifle against his temple.

"That's far enough. Get your hands in the air and turn off the machine."

Slowly Aaron killed the engine and raised his hands. He'd failed. Would it end up costing Liz her life?

FIVE

It was up to her now. Liz steeled herself for what she must do.

The men guarding her had begun to talk amongst themselves. With the boss gone, their attention was distracted. She guessed they figured she wasn't going anywhere.

Liz started back on the knot working as quickly as she could. It felt like she'd been working it for hours when the rope finally loosened enough so that she could slip first one hand and then the other free. Her battered wrist was almost numb from the restraints. She flexed her fingers and pins and needles shot through her hand.

Time was critical and Aaron needed her help. She couldn't afford to wait any longer. Still, her bound legs presented another problem entirely. She couldn't loosen the ties around them without drawing attention to herself.

Now if she could convince one of the men she was in distress and get him to come close enough, she could disarm him, and hopefully take down the two remaining soldiers. The only variable was Rick. She hadn't seen him in a while, but suspected he was around somewhere.

Please, Lord, I need Your help, Liz prayed earnestly then let out a strangled cry and slumped over in her chair, her eyes closed.

"What's wrong with her?" one of the men asked in a worried tone. Liz didn't move a muscle. She had to convince them she was in distress.

"I don't know—maybe it's the drugs they used on her. But if *he* comes back and finds her dead without him having ordered it, there'll be trouble for all of us. Go check on her."

One of the men rushed to her side. This was it. Her pulse exploded with adrenaline.

"Hey, wake up," the man barked and stopped within inches. When she didn't respond, he leaned over her and felt for a pulse. His gun was slung over one shoulder, just within her reach.

Liz snatched the weapon and then head-butted the man with all her strength. He turned toward his partners, staggering as if trying to keep his footing. While she saw stars from the impact, she jumped up, her feet still bound.

Grabbing the man from behind, Liz pulled him close. One of the other men ran for her. She took the stock of the weapon and slammed it against the charging man's head. He dropped to the floor unconscious. The remaining guard ran for the door.

"That's far enough," she yelled and he stopped dead. "Drop the weapon and get your hands in the air."

The man hesitated with his back still to her.

"Do it now," she ordered.

"She's hurt. You can take her," the one she'd restrained urged his partner. Buoyed by his friend's urgings, the man charged her and the man she'd subdued jerked free and quickly moved out of her reach.

Before she could move, the charging man knocked her over. Pain shot from her damaged wrist and it felt as if her bruised ribs were reinjured.

The man wrestled for control of the assault rifle and she was quickly losing ground. Liz became aware of a door opening as she fought with all her strength to free herself from the man on top of her.

Someone yelled in pain. Rick came into her line of sight. He had his weapon held high above his head in a defensive gesture. Liz barely got out the word *no*, when Rick slammed his gun against the guy's head and he slumped on top of her, out cold.

Rick hauled the unconscious man off Liz and over to where he'd knocked out the man she'd held on to.

While he secured the three men, she grabbed the gun she'd lost in the struggle and got to her feet.

Rick came back to Liz and untied her legs. Immediately, she turned the rifle on him.

"Drop the weapon," Liz breathed unsteadily. The shooting pain down her ribs made speaking normally impossible. He slowly lowered the weapon and raised his hands.

"I'm not going to hurt you," he said.

"Kick your weapon over here." She waited until the man begrudgingly did as she asked. "Now do the same with his." She pointed to the unconscious man and he shoved the weapon to Liz.

She slid both of the guns as far out of the men's reach as she could. Just the slightest of movements greatly depleted her strength.

"Let me help you. You're hurt," Rick urged. She didn't believe him for a second. Not after he'd drugged both her and Aaron. "Get down on the floor and put your hands behind your back," she commanded.

Once he'd done as she requested, she did a quick search of Rick's and the other men's pockets, taking their phones. Liz spotted hers and Aaron's Glocks along with her backpack on the kitchen table. She tucked the handguns behind her back before hurrying to the window. She couldn't see anyone else around. Still, she couldn't risk the men calling out for help after she was gone so she gagged everyone but Rick. She needed answers from him.

"Please, don't leave me here with them," Rick begged and they stared at each other for a breath.

"I'm sorry," he whispered in a broken tone,

his face contorted in pain. While she believed he meant it, she still didn't trust him. First he'd double-crossed Michael, and then he'd betrayed them. "They'll kill me if you leave me here. They were just using me to get to you," he insisted, grabbing her full attention.

"Then why'd you betray your friend? Michael trusted you and you double-crossed him."

His face crumpled in pain. "You don't understand. They have my family. They said they were going to kill them if I didn't do exactly as they asked."

Stunned, she stared at him in astonishment. As much as she wanted to know more about the threat used against Rick's family, Aaron's life was in danger. "Then help me. Once they find out Aaron's bluffing, they'll kill him."

Rick willingly agreed. "Of course. Just tell me what you need. I hate what I've done and Michael's a good friend. I'm sorry I let him down."

Was he playing her? She prayed not because right now she needed his help. "Aaron's taking them to the airstrip. We need to get there before they do."

He nodded. "I know a shortcut. If we take the Cat, we'll get there quicker." He hesitated. "I'll need a weapon…"

She shook her head. "You'll get it once we're there. Until then, I don't trust you at all." As much as she wanted his help, she wasn't about to let her guard down for a second. Liz grabbed up the assault rifles from the floor and then her backpack and pointed to the door. "You go first. Don't try anything because I won't hesitate to shoot if you do."

Liz gathered all three of the men's assault rifles and took them with her. She had a feeling both she and Aaron would need the extra weaponry and so would Rick.

"Let's go," she said once they reached the Sno-Cat.

Rick climbed into the vehicle and she followed, carefully glancing around to make sure there were no others there.

If he were telling the truth, she couldn't imagine how terrifying it must be knowing your family was being held hostage and one false move could end their lives.

Liz knew how merciless these people were. There was a very real chance that even if Rick did help them, they might still kill his family because they could identify who'd kidnapped them.

Rick started up the engine. "You'd better hang on to something. The route we're taking is a difficult one." He headed the machine off in the direction of the small hill behind the house where he'd told them he stored a spare snowmobile.

"How far is it?" she asked suspiciously as they bounced over tree stumps and downed branches.

"Not far. Maybe about a mile. It's almost twice that distance the way they're going."

"Meaning we should arrive first."

He spared her a look. "That's right. We should have enough time to get into position before they arrive. The snowmobiles put out a lot of noise so they shouldn't hear the Cat unless they stop for any reason."

"Where will this route bring us out at?" she asked. "The airstrip butts up to the woods, as I recall."

Rick kept his gaze locked on the horizon in front of them. "That's correct. It will be the perfect place to leave the vehicle. They won't know we're there, which means we should be able to take them by surprise."

Up ahead, she could see the lights of the airstrip coming into view. They were close.

Rick veered off to the left. Putting a hill between them and the airstrip, he then killed the engine.

Silence permeated the cab and Liz listened intently. "I don't hear anything yet," she said and turned so that she could study his profile carefully.

Rick glanced her way. "I don't either, but they should be here soon enough. If we can reach the back of the hangar, it'll provide us with cover. They won't be able to see us until we rush them. We'll have the element of surprise."

It made sense and under different circumstances she would have believed him, but after the things she and Aaron had gone through recently...

By all indications, Michael, the person she'd trusted in the past, had betrayed her. Then Rick had drugged them and allowed them to be captured. She thought about what the leader said about the weapons. How had they known about Black Bear? The only explanation was that Michael had told them.

How deep had Michael been involved in Sam's crimes? Had he been working for Sam all along, even while she and Michael were being held captive in Afghanistan before Sam had brought them to the US and before that fateful crash in Pennsylvania?

Another disturbing thought occurred. Had Michael been part of the kidnapping? The team had wondered how Sam had been able to transport two agents into US airspace without detection. If Michael was part of Sam's organization, he could have somehow cleared the way.

Liz let go of those upsetting ideas. She hated thinking of Michael's part in the crimes. "We need to hurry. We won't have much time." She slung one of the rifles over her shoulder and got out. Rick followed a second later.

Liz shoved aside her misgivings at trusting Rick and prayed he wouldn't expose her once the men arrived.

They climbed to the top of the hill. Ducking low, Liz could see Aaron's plane and the rest of the airstrip beyond the hangars. Other than that, the place appeared deserted.

Shouldn't they be close by now? Another frightening thought occurred. What if the leader had lied and had taken Aaron away to kill him?

With all her heart, she prayed for Aaron's safety and let go of those doubts. She had to keep a clear head if she and Aaron were going to get through this alive.

She studied the layout of the airstrip. If they could reach the back side of the hangars, they'd have an advantage if Aaron could get them to the plane. There were so many variables at play.

Liz pointed to the back of the hangars. "We need to be there," she told Rick and he nodded.

Slowly they eased from their vantage point and hurried to the back. Once they reached the buildings, she unstrapped the extra gun, put in the clip and handed it to Rick.

"Thank you," he said humbly.

"Don't thank me. Just help me save his life."

Aaron's head throbbed from the blow he'd taken that had knocked him unconscious.

"Do you want me to kill him?" someone close by asked and then kicked his side.

"No, there might still be the chance he actually knows where the weapons are. Safar's mad enough as it is. If we don't find them soon, it'll mean our heads."

Aaron recognized the leader's voice. He focused on the name mentioned. Safar. It didn't ring any bells, but he had no doubt this was the real person in charge and the one responsible for killing both Michael and Sam. Was it possible he was a new name amongst the terrorists? He didn't believe it. He obviously had ties to Sam.

"This time, tie his hands until we reach the airstrip. I don't want a repeat of what happened here."

Someone knelt next to him and slapped him hard. Aaron opened his eyes slowly and stared into the face of pure evil.

"Are you done playing games?" the man growled and motioned to one of the men who hauled him to his feet.

The leader got to within inches of Aaron's face. "You'll pay dearly for what you just did, I promise you."

The one holding his arm jerked Aaron toward the buried snowmobile. "Get it out," he ordered.

Even though his head ached and he struggled to keep the bile away, Aaron went to work unburying the snowmobile. By the time he'd finished he was sweating profusely. The cold air chilled him to the bone. It wouldn't take long under the circumstances for hypothermia to set in. He prayed Liz had managed to free herself and subdue the men guarding her.

Keep her safe, he prayed silently.

"Let's go. We've wasted enough time as it is. *He's* expecting results," the leader snapped.

One of the men bound Aaron's hands behind his back and forced him on the machine to the rear of him while the leader and the second man waited.

It took all of Aaron's strength to stay on the machine as the man roared down the trail, dodging trees along the way.

As they drew near, Aaron searched the surrounding area, but there was no sign of Liz. What if she hadn't been able to escape? Or worse. He pushed those disparaging thoughts aside. He had to stay focused.

Once they reached the airstrip, instead of going to his plane as Aaron had expected, the driver headed for a nearby hangar. The men had no intention of using Aaron's plane.

Uneasiness slithered down his spine. Would Liz make it in time? Or had everything he'd done so far been in vain. Was Liz dead already? The very thought ripped his heart to shreds.

SIX

In the distance, the noise of snowmobiles could be heard coming their way.

"Why is it taking them so long?" she turned and asked Rick while carefully studying his expression. Was he up to something?

She handed him the binoculars she'd brought with her. He seemed genuinely concerned as he looked through the lenses. "There." He pointed off to the right. "I see them. They're almost here." Liz tucked close to the back of the hangar and Rick followed her lead.

Once the vehicles came to a stop, she heard the man in charge yelling.

"Untie him," the leader ordered one of his men. Silence followed and then he said, "You will tell me where the weapons are now, before we go anywhere. And if you're bluffing, she's dead." The man's voice grew louder. They were moving their way.

Close by, an overhead door swung open and

tension burned inside her stomach. They weren't heading for Aaron's plane.

She swung to face Rick. "What's going on?" she demanded.

He shook his head, as confused as she was by the turn of events. "I don't know."

"What's in that hangar?" she asked, still not fully trusting him.

He didn't hesitate. "The plane they flew in on."

As Liz listened carefully, she just heard Aaron's response.

"They should be exactly where we left them unless your partner Rick moved them."

A lengthy hesitation was followed by, "Liar." The leader was growing more suspicious. "Call the rest of the team. Have them bring her here. He's useless. He knows nothing. Take him into the woods and kill him."

If they made that call, they'd know something was wrong. With Aaron's life in grave danger, it was now or never.

"He can't stall them any longer," she whispered. "We have to move now". Liz edged toward the entrance of the hangar with Rick close behind.

"On my count," she whispered and then counted off three. When the final number was out, she and Rick charged the hangar taking everyone by surprise.

Aaron immediately realized what was happening and leaped into action. He shoved an elbow into the leader's gut while he was still distracted. The man doubled over in pain and Aaron whipped around to disarm him, but the man fought back.

Liz rushed to aid Aaron, but another man stepped between and lunged for her. There was no time to get a shot off before he was right on top of her. Bracing the assault rifle in front of her she began using it as a hand-to-hand combat weapon, slamming it hard into the man's side. He doubled over in pain, spouting angry words her way.

Before she had time to regroup, a second man lunged forward with his weapon aimed at her head. She squeezed her eyes shut. A shot echoed through the enclosed building doubling the noise, yet nothing happened. Her eyes flew open. The man's look of shock would be forever branded in her head. He dropped to his knees in front of her. Blood oozed through his shirt, quickly staining it as he slumped to the floor.

She was alive. It took a second for her brain to assimilate that truth. Relief threatened to buckle her knees.

Aaron rushed to her, his hands framing her face. "Are you okay?" he asked frantically, misconstruing her reaction for injury. She could feel the color drain from her face. She'd almost died.

She slowly nodded. "I'm okay. Thank you, Aaron. You saved my life."

He brought her close and hugged her tight. "It

wasn't me," he whispered against her hair then let her go and looked over at Rick.

Shocked, Liz faced the man who had come to her aid. Rick looked just as surprised as she by what had happened.

Aaron went over and took the weapon from his unresisting hands. "Thank you for saving Liz, but that still doesn't let you off the hook for what you've done."

He bowed his head. "Yes, what I did was wrong, but they have Melinda and my daughters. They said they'd kill them if I didn't do exactly what they said."

The revelation was clearly surprising to Aaron. "Is this the guy who took your family?" He indicated the leader he'd disarmed.

Rick stared at the man, still clearly afraid of him. Rick swallowed nervously and Aaron motioned him a little away from the men and out of earshot.

"You'd better tell us everything," Aaron said.

Rick blew out a breath and nodded. "When he and his men first arrived, he was ranting crazily. He roughed me up and forced me back to the cabin. There he told me that someone from the CIA's Scorpion team had stolen weapons intended for a different use, and that he wanted them back. I had no idea what he was talking about, only that I remembered Michael had mentioned working for the CIA. I assumed it was somehow connected to him."

Aaron's gaze slipped to Liz. "Did he mention Michael by name?"

Rick shook his head. "No, never. Just that someone had betrayed him."

Aaron told Liz about overhearing the name Safar.

She shook her head. "You think it's the real person in charge?"

"Probably," Aaron said with a nod. "We need to find out who is behind this thing and we need to do it now. We're running out of time."

Liz handed Aaron his Glock and he went over to the man who was the leader and squatted next to him. "If you want a chance to live out your life, you'd better tell us who you're working for."

The man stared at Aaron with venom. "I'm not telling you anything and you're a dead man…and so is your family," he shouted to Rick who turned pale as a sheet and flinched.

"Keep your mouth shut," Aaron ordered the man and then got to his feet and went back to Rick.

"What else is there, Rick?" Aaron said. "Right now you're in serious trouble and facing federal charges. So if there's more, being honest is the only thing that will save your family and keep you out of prison."

* * *

Aaron owed her his life. If Liz hadn't managed to escape when she had, he'd be dead, no doubt about it. She never ceased to amaze him. She had that rare combination of bravery and compassion that helped her excel at her job and in life. As he looked at her now, he realized how important she'd become to him. He wasn't sure when it had happened, or maybe he just hadn't wanted to acknowledge it, but Liz meant more to him than just a friend and he wasn't about to let anything happen to her on his watch. To clear her name, they needed answers more than anything else. He was certain Rick could help them fill in some of the pieces.

Aaron stared at Rick's devastated expression and was eye witness to the turmoil he'd gone through knowing that to save his family he'd have to betray his friend.

Aaron glanced up at the sky. The snow had eased somewhat. The weather was letting up. They'd need to be on their way soon if they stood a chance at reaching Black Bear by nightfall.

"Let's talk at the cabin. We need to get these guys back and restrained as soon as possible. The weather seems to be lifting. We need to be airborne," he told Liz.

"I'll take one of the prisoners with me. Rick, if you can drive the other snowmobile we can get them both out of sight in case someone else shows up here."

Aaron turned to Liz. As a pilot, he knew she could handle the Sno-Cat under normal circumstances, but she was still recovering from her injuries. "Think you can get this thing back to the cabin with the rest of the prisoners?"

She didn't hesitate. "I'm certain of it. Let's make sure they're secured so that they can't try anything."

Once the two men were restrained and loaded into the Cat with Liz, Aaron bound his prisoner's hands behind his back and got him on the machine. With Rick ahead of him, they followed behind Liz in case she ran into a problem. As they eased along, Aaron tried to make sense of everything that happened. His head throbbed from the blow.

The leader had said that the weapons weren't in Black Bear, which seemed to indicate that had been the delivery location. Something had gone wrong, though. With Michael's connection to the Alaskan village undeniable, there was little doubt that he was involved in Sam's deception somehow.

Aaron struggled with the best way to help Rick's family. He'd need Jase's help to rescue them safely, but if he contacted his friend, he'd be giving away their location. He'd already disobeyed a direct order. In his mind, there was only one option.

Once they reached the cabin, Liz and Aaron took all the men to the bedroom and tied them together. They needed to know exactly what had happened before the kidnapping took place, if they stood a chance at bringing Rick's family back safely.

"Let's talk outside and out of their hearing," Liz told him as if reading his thoughts. He nodded and all three of them went out into cold morning. Once they were out of earshot, Aaron stopped.

"We don't have much time, Rick. The men holding your family will start to get antsy if they don't hear from these guys soon. We need to know everything about your relationship with Michael and what he told you about the missing weapons."

Aaron glanced over at Liz. He could tell she still didn't trust Rick any more than he did.

Rick slowly nodded, all but confirming he at least knew something about Michael's crimes.

He gathered his breath. "I was telling you the truth about how I met Michael. He found my ad in a fishing magazine and called me up. He was nice. I liked him a lot and we hit it off right away. As I said, that was a few years back and we've become good friends since."

"How often did he hire you to take him to Black Bear?" Aaron asked because he wanted to know if Rick was being honest about everything. He'd heard Michael talk about fishing there enough to know how often he went.

"Usually a couple of times a year," Rick told him and Aaron's gaze slid to Liz. She briefly nodded. That number matched what she knew to be true as well.

"Tell us about the last call you had with Michael. The one that brought you here," Liz asked without mentioning Michael's fate.

Rick hesitated and all of Aaron's suspicions doubled. "What is it?" he prompted.

He shook his head. "I'm not sure. There was just something odd in his voice when he called. Michael was always so upbeat in the past, but this time, well, it was as if the weight of the world was on his shoulders and he whispered a lot, as if he were trying to keep someone from hearing him."

Liz sucked in a breath. "When was this exactly?" she asked and Aaron wondered why.

"A little over two weeks ago. I hadn't heard from him in a few months so I was happy that he called, but when he started to speak, I knew something was wrong right away."

Aaron noticed the alarm on Liz's face and asked, "What is it?"

"That's around the same time Michael and I were taken," she told him and he could see there was something else that troubled her.

Rick immediately picked up on what she'd said. "Wait, is Michael okay?"

Aaron ignored the man's question for the moment. He still didn't trust Rick fully and because of it, he wasn't ready to divulge the truth about Michael's death. "Did something unusual happen during that time?" he asked Liz.

She slowly nodded. "It did. At the time I didn't think much about it because everything that happened was so terrifying and I was sure Sam would kill us both."

Aaron watched as she recalled the disturbing memory. "Once we arrived in the US, we were held at the abandoned lumber mill in Pennsylvania. Most of the time we were blindfolded, but shortly after we arrived, Michael was taken away for almost the entire day. When he came back, I could tell something significant had occurred. When I asked him about it, he told me they'd tried to get information about Scorpion headquarters out of him. He said the interrogation had been brutal and yet later on, I didn't see any fresh wounds on his person."

"You think it was a lie," Aaron concluded. "Michael must have arranged to have the weapons flown out of the area at that time, but something obviously went wrong because they didn't end up in Black Bear."

Did Michael have a change of heart and move the weapons somewhere out of the buyer's reach?

Why hadn't Liz mentioned this detail before now? Had it truly slipped her mind or was she covering for someone?

With difficulty, he shoved aside his misgivings.

He knew Liz. She wasn't involved in Sam's or Michael's crimes.

He turned to Rick. "What else did Michael tell you?" So far, all they had was a bunch of speculation.

"He said he needed me to come here. He called and told me that there were going to be several planes flying into the airstrip and that I was to store their cargo in my hangars until he got in touch with me again. That's why I'm here now. I'm waiting for him. Only nothing happened. Michael never showed." Rick lifted his shoulders.

"It has to be the missing weapons," Liz said. "But they never reached Black Bear. At least not at the location they were expecting them to be. So what happened to them?"

Aaron had a theory. "I'm thinking something scared Michael into switching his plans. Most likely he was worried what would happen once they reached the hands of the intended buyer."

Still, something about Rick's story didn't add up in Aaron's mind. "You said you've been here for over two weeks?" The man nodded. "Then when did these men take your family hostage?"

There was no way they'd been held all that time. It would have caused too many red flags if the family's daily life was disrupted for such a long period of time. The daughters would be missed at school and if the wife worked there would be people looking for her by now.

"A few days ago. I stayed here because there was work to do on the cabin and, well, I was worried about Michael. I'd tried to reach him numerous times but he didn't answer. I wanted to be here in case he showed."

Aaron eyed him suspiciously. "I checked his phone. There've been no calls from you, Rick. Either you called a different number or you're lying."

Rick was clearly confused. "I have his number right here. It's the same number I've used to reach him for a while now. When these guys showed, I thought they were the ones Michael talked about, until they drew down on me and forced me back to the cabin. Then they told me what they'd done to my family." Rick stopped, drawing in a much-needed breath.

"Needless to say, I was terrified for my family. I told them I wasn't doing anything until they let me speak to my wife. They called her phone. Only it wasn't her that answered. It was some guy with an accent. He said I'd better do what they asked or my family would die. I was terrified. I thought…well, I thought they might have killed them already so I asked to speak with Melinda again." He paused for a moment. Aaron could see the conversation had been a difficult one.

"They finally put her on the phone and she told me that they were okay, but that the men had barged into our house, taken their phones and tied them up. The man took the phone from Melinda.

He stated that they would tell me what to do when the time came."

He looked up at Aaron. "It was almost as if they were expecting you to come here because as soon as you texted, these guys gave me the drugs that knocked you unconscious. They took off on the snowmobiles so you wouldn't suspect anything. After they left, I tried to reach Michael. I wanted to see if he could help me, but…" He lifted his shoulders and then handed Aaron his phone. "Here's the number I used to contact Michael."

Aaron didn't recognize it.

He showed it to Liz. "It's his burner," she confirmed.

"Wait, you knew about this number?" Aaron asked uneasily and wasn't able to hide it.

"Aaron, we were partners," she said, obviously hurt by his doubt. "He knew mine as well. After the kidnapping and crash, we wanted to have another means of getting in touch with each other."

It made sense, so why didn't it sit well with him? "What happened next?" he asked Rick without answering Liz.

The man shook his head. "They just got here before the storm blew in. As I said, I saw the plane coming in and thought it must be the people Michael talked about, so I came out to help. Then you called and said you were coming. When I told them, they seemed pleased." Rick blew out a sigh. "I guess they were expecting the drug to act faster because when they showed up at the cabin, they were surprised that you were still conscious."

"They must have known about your connection to Michael somehow. It's the only explanation," Liz said.

"I guess so, but how? Where is Michael anyway? Is he in some kind of trouble?" Rick's gaze skidded between them. He must have sensed something was wrong. "What is it? Is he okay?"

Aaron blew out a breath. "He's dead. Michael was murdered, Rick. Probably by someone connected to these guys. I'm guessing the man with the accent."

Rick's mouth fell open. He stared wide-eyed at Aaron as if not fully understanding. "Murdered. You're kidding… I can't believe it." He shook his head. "He was my friend. I would have done anything for him. I can't believe it."

The man's grief wasn't faked. Rick was a good man who'd been forced into an impossible situation by a bunch of thugs. Unfortunately, they were still no closer to knowing who was behind Michael's and Sam's murders or where the missing weapons were and time was running out on Rick's family.

"I can't explain how they knew about the cabin or my friendship with Michael for that matter. But please, you've got to help me. If they killed him, they won't hesitate to do the same to my wife and kids. They can't afford to leave any witnesses behind," Rick choked out.

Aaron's heart went out to the man. He couldn't imagine having to make such a difficult decision. "We will help you," he assured Rick and then turned to Liz. "We have to loop Jase in on what's happened here." He took her arm and they stepped a little away from Rick.

"Liz, we don't have a choice anymore," he said quietly. "His family is in danger. They'll die if we don't help them. If these guys know about Rick's connection to Michael, then they probably know about the cabin and Jessie Chena could be in danger as well." He stopped for a second. "We have to prepare ourselves. They may have the evidence already."

The desperation etched on every square inch of her pretty face shredded his heart. "No, I can't even think about that happening," she somehow got the words out. He knew what was coming next. "I'm sorry, Aaron, but I won't go back to Painted Rock without first trying everything in my power to find out who's behind Michael's murder. I'm sure not trusting my freedom or my life to anyone else but you."

She squared her shoulders and looked him in the eye. "If you can't help me, I understand. I'll find another way there. I don't have a choice."

Her passion didn't surprise him. It was one of things that he'd always admired about her. Her overwhelming dedication to a cause. To her deceased husband Eric.

He smiled. "You know I'll help you. I'll do whatever it takes to clear your name."

The gratitude in her eyes tightened his chest. She was so beautiful. He'd always known this, yet with the two of them facing unknown dangers, running for their lives, well, it was as if his eyes had been opened. He was seeing her as more than just a subordinate and it scared him. He couldn't go there again, surely. Beth's betrayal still cut deep.

He prayed the proof Liz so desperately needed was real and not just Michael sending her on a wild-goose chase to cover up his crimes.

"But we still need to let Jase know what's happened here. It's relevant to the case and it could help clear your name. I'll find a way to loop him in without telling him where we are."

She didn't argue and they went back over to where Rick was.

"When you spoke to your wife, did she give you any indication how many men are watching them?" When Jase dispatched SWAT to rescue his family, they'd need to know what they were up against.

Rick hesitated. "I'm not sure. As I said, she couldn't really talk. I got the impression they were standing right on top of her. But she did keep mentioning our eldest daughter's sixth birthday party.

Do you think she might have been trying to tell me something by that?"

"It sounds like it," Aaron said. "You said one of the men had an accent. Could you recognize it again?"

"Maybe," Rick said.

"Do you have any idea where the closest trooper station is?" Aaron asked. They'd need to have troopers pick up these men as soon as possible.

"Probably Wasilla. They closed the station near Talkeetna a few years back."

"That's a good hour away." Aaron glanced up at the sky. The snow had begun to fall again. If they stood a chance at getting out, they'd need to be on their way soon. Aaron grabbed his cell and called the state troopers. Once he'd identified himself and explained what had happened, the colonel in charge assured him he would dispatch men right away.

Rick cast a worried glance at the falling snow. "I'd better check the forecast and see what's coming this way." He excused himself and hurried inside. Liz and Aaron followed.

The restrained men hadn't moved, but the leader glared at Aaron when he and Liz checked on them.

Once Aaron closed the door, Liz motioned him to the kitchen area. "There's no way these men are the ones who killed Michael and Sam and they certainly weren't the ones who tried to kill us earlier. The real killer is still out there somewhere. Probably this Safar person."

He had to agree. "From the amount of weapons we suspect may have gone missing, whoever is behind this has shelled out a lot of money for them and they won't give up until they have them."

Aaron racked his brain trying to come up with a way to let Jase know what had happened without giving away their location.

He glanced back at the closed bedroom door. "I don't like leaving Rick here alone with those thugs. If they somehow managed to get free, they'd kill him."

Liz touched his arm. "I know, but we may not have a choice. The weather's building again and we need to get to Black Bear as soon as possible. We don't have much time. Especially once Jase knows about what happened here."

She was right. Still, until they knew for certain who was behind the murders and the attacks, they couldn't let down their guard. The more time the information Michael left at the cabin was unattended, the bigger the chance someone would stumble on it.

Rick returned with a grim look on his face. "There's a bad front moving in behind this last one. You guys need to get out of here while you still can."

With no other option, Aaron said, "I'm going to give you a number to call once Liz and I are gone.

The man's name is Jase Bradford. He's CIA and you can trust him. Tell him everything that happened to your family and here. He can help rescue your wife and children." He hesitated. "I just need you not to mention ever seeing us."

Rick stared at him for the longest time before agreeing. "I understand. You were never here."

Aaron glanced Liz's way. He could see she was relieved with his decision not to call Jase even though it meant they were both, in a sense, fugitives. "We need to hurry. We don't want to miss our window."

"Thank you both so much," Rick said with heartfelt gratitude. "And I'm sorry for what I put you through. I wish there had been a different way out. I just don't want to lose my family."

Liz took his hand. "If my family had been in the same situation, I would have done what you did. The troopers should be here soon. In the meantime, keep an eye on those guys."

Rick nodded. "I will. Take the Cat. It'll get you there quicker. Do you think they'll be looking for your plane?"

Aaron hadn't thought about it. "It's a possibility."

"Then take my Challenger. It's fueled and ready and if you run into any bad weather, it's more stable."

Rick was right. The Challenger was bigger and heavier. It could withstand a whole lot more than his plane. "Thanks, Rick. I'll get it back to you as soon as possible. Take care of yourself."

Once they reached the airstrip, he and Liz worked quickly to get the Challenger out of its hangar and ready for flight. Precious time had slipped away and Black Bear was still several hours ahead of them. It would be dark by the time they reached the village.

"I hope Rick keeps his word and doesn't mention us to Jase," Liz said the second the plane was safely in the air.

Aaron had believed the man had been sincere. "I think he will, but Jase is a smart man. He'll put two and two together and figure out we were involved. At least we've managed to buy ourselves some time. I just hope that evidence is where Michael said it would be, otherwise we're both in a lot of trouble."

She squeezed his arm. "Thank you. I know this isn't easy for you. I'm so sorry I got you involved."

He shook his head. "No, you don't have any reason to be sorry. You didn't ask for any of this to happen." He smiled tenderly at her. "I'd do anything for you, Liz. I…care about you." He caught himself before he said something more. "You know that, don't you?"

"I do. I really do." She leaned over and kissed his cheek and he could feel his pulse responding to her touch. Everything they'd gone through and whatever they faced in the future would be worth the trust she'd placed in him.

With hours of travel time still ahead of them, Aaron chewed on what had happened at Rick's, trying to get it to make sense. One thing in particular gnawed at him.

How did those men know Rick would be in the area? There was no way it had been an accident that they showed up when Rick was there, or that they knew about his family. The thought played uneasily through his head. They had been to Black Bear. Had they found out Michael's connection to the village? If so, was the trip to Black Bear a setup?

"You think they'll be there waiting for us?" she asked as if reading his thoughts.

He wished he had a definitive answer, but he had no idea what they'd be facing. Either the real man in charge would be there with more armed men, or the evidence Michael had left there would be long gone along with the men and Liz's last chance at freedom.

SEVEN

The Challenger came to a bone-jarring stop on the tiny landing strip Rick had told them about some distance outside of Black Bear, Alaska.

Liz glanced uneasily around. Nothing about the place was welcoming. Rick had said it was isolated and that the man on duty was a friend. He assured them the guy could provide them with a snowmobile for the rest of the journey into town. From there, it would be up to them to find Jessie Chena and get to Michael's cabin.

She just hoped that she hadn't put Aaron's life in danger as well as her own for something that never existed. She had a sinking feeling that Michael may have sent them on a wild-goose chase.

The desolation of their surroundings did little to settle her nerves. There was nothing but a small metal building serving as an office, and a couple of fuel pumps off to one side...then wilderness.

Never having been to Alaska before, she thought Michael had painted a far more hospitable picture when he'd spoken fondly of the area. Yet nothing about the ruggedness of the landscape was encouraging. She couldn't imagine living in such a remote place.

"We should refuel while we're here just in case we have to leave quickly," Aaron said and Liz knew exactly what he meant. They had no idea what they'd be facing.

She squinted at the building but couldn't tell if anyone was in the office. "Do you think it's closed?" she asked after they'd gotten out.

More than ten hours had passed since they'd left Colorado and night was closing in quickly. They'd be forced to make their way the rest of the distance to the village in darkness. Not knowing the landscape, they could end up running off the side of the mountain or burying the machine.

Aaron glanced that direction. "I can't tell, but I sure hope not, because we need a means of traveling cross-country. We have to find Jessie Chena and then get to the cabin, find the box and get back to the plane as fast as possible."

Liz stretched the kinks from her back. The pain in her ribs had increased tenfold. And she was pretty sure her wrist was swelling dangerously by the minute. Disarming those men had taken its toll.

"How are you holding up?" Aaron asked softly and she realized he'd seen the pain she was in.

"I'm fine," she forced out and hoped he didn't

see it for the lie it was. Not that it mattered. They were all out of choices. Like it or not, they had to keep pushing on. Without the evidence she couldn't clear her name. She'd face prison, or worse, die because someone believed she had a part in stealing the weapons.

Aaron reached for her hand, stopping her before she could head for the office. She turned to him, reading all of his worry in the taut set of his jaw. She shook her head. What good did it do to talk about it? It was what it was.

"Hey." He pulled her toward him. "How are you, really?"

Liz closed her eyes. She wondered how she'd been so blessed to deserve his friendship. Would she feel the same way if the tables were turned? The tenderness in his tone was something she didn't deserve. He was risking everything to save her. She'd stay strong. Endure the pain to do her part.

She smiled again and meant it. "I'm holding up." She stepped closer, inches from him. He was strong and courageous and she could no longer deny she had feelings for him. "We'll get through this, Aaron."

He looked deep into her eyes and slowly returned her smile. "Yes. We will."

The promise she saw in him had her looking away. In so many ways, Aaron reminded her of Eric. She'd loved Eric so much. At times, she'd remember something they'd done together and it brought home the loss. She'd almost forgotten how lonely life was without him. But she couldn't imagine loving another man the way she had Eric. The pain was just too great.

Aaron's gaze narrowed as he continued to watch the sadness she couldn't begin to hide from him.

"What is it?" he asked and she shook her head when she couldn't answer.

With her hand still in his, they headed for the office. As they drew closer, Liz noticed a man watching them through the grimy glass front. "That must be Rick's friend." She nodded to the man in the window.

Aaron's stride hiccuped. "I hope we can trust Rick's judgment on this guy." He shot her a worried look. "I get he was only trying to save his family, but how does the old saying go—once burned twice wary? With the things that have happened so far, I'm beyond wary."

Liz squeezed his hand. "I know. I find myself second-guessing it all. Still, I can't imagine what Rick went through. He was caught in an impossible situation and had to make that choice. Do you think his family will be okay?" She had a feeling Rick's terror wasn't anywhere close to being over.

"I hope so. If Rick loses his family because he helped us..." He didn't finish, but she understood. It would be unthinkable if more innocent lives were lost to these people.

"With Jase's help his family will be okay. He will make sure they're safe," she told him and then prayed it would be true.

"We'd better go inside before this old guy gets any more suspicious. I doubt that he sees a lot of new people around these parts."

Liz smiled at Aaron's attempt to lighten the tension.

"Evening, folks. Can I help you with something?" the old man asked when they stepped inside. While he appeared innocent enough, the past few days had taught her that bad people sometimes came in innocent packages.

The man was midsixties and rail thin. His hair was thinning on top and he peered at them over thick Coke-bottle glasses.

"Rick Evans told us that you might be able to help us with some transportation," Aaron said and waited for the man to blink.

The man stared at them suspiciously for an uncomfortable length of time. "That so? You two friends of Rick, you say? I thought that looked like his Challenger."

Aaron nodded. "That's right. Rick let us borrow it for this trip. We were just at his place."

The man glanced from Aaron to Liz then relaxed visibly. "Name's Everett Sanford," he said and held out his hand for Aaron to shake. "Rick's a good man. He stops by from time to time to bring me some special coffee they make in Seattle."

Aaron smiled in agreement. "That sounds like Rick."

"Well, I rent out snowmobiles on occasion to hunters. You two know how to use a snowmobile?" he asked curiously.

"We do," Liz assured him.

"You guys coming to Black Bear for the hunting?"

The man was full of questions, she thought. But then again, he probably didn't see a lot of people.

Liz reined in her frustration and nodded. "Rick told us this is a good place for it."

"Oh my, yes. It's world famous so you've come to the right place." He scratched his head. "But I only have one machine left. Rented the others out a few days earlier. Will that work?"

Liz glanced at Aaron. "There are other hunters in the area?"

"Yep, a bunch of city slickers from the lower forty-eight came in a few days ago in some choppers. They said they were heading to Black Bear." The elder man glanced out the window at the fading light. "You guys had better hurry if you want to reach Black Bear tonight. It'll be dark soon and the temperature here gets pretty ugly." The man opened a drawer and brought out a set of keys.

Liz couldn't afford to ask more questions. If

the man was working for the enemy she couldn't risk alarming him.

Aaron took the keys. "Thanks. How much do we owe you?" He clasped her uninjured hand as if signaling to tread carefully.

"We'll settle up when you return," the man volunteered. In their line of work it was hard to trust anyone. Was this man simply being kind or did he have ulterior motives?

"Is it okay if I leave the plane here until we get back?" Aaron asked and the man nodded his head. "I'll need to refuel it before we go."

"I can do that for you. It's usually pretty quiet around here. It'll give me something to do. How long you folks going to be in Black Bear?"

Liz had no idea what they'd be facing once they reached the village. What if Jessie wasn't around anymore? The thought was terrifying.

"Probably only a few days, if that's okay?" Aaron asked.

The elder man nodded. "That's no problem. I'll take care of refueling your plane. The snowmobile's around back. You two be careful now."

Once they were outside and out of earshot, Liz voiced her concerns. "Do you think the men he was talking about are the same ones looking for the weapons?"

She could see that Aaron had come to the same conclusion. "I'd say it's a good possibility. We have to try to stay off their radar until we find out for sure." He crooked his thumb toward the office. "This guy seems harmless enough, but he sure likes to talk, which isn't a good thing should the wrong people stop by and ask questions."

"I was afraid he might be working for those men," she said and suppressed shudder.

Aaron stopped. "Me too. It's sad when kindness draws suspicion, isn't it."

He was right. "Maybe we've been at this too long. We're becoming jaded."

He looked deep into her eyes and her breath hung in her chest. "I've forgotten what it's like to live like normal people without having to look over your shoulder or worry that everyone you meet might be the enemy."

Liz couldn't imagine a time when she wouldn't have to be suspicious of everything. She'd been with the CIA since she'd graduated from Langley Flying School. At one time it was all she thought about. She ate, slept and breathed the job. But when she'd lost Eric, the bottom had fallen out of her world. She realized how precious life was and how quickly happiness could fade. She'd thought she and Eric would grow old together. They'd made plans to one day buy a ranch with lots of land to spread out. They'd talked about it right before Eric left on his final mission, never realizing it would be their last time together.

If she were being honest, the danger they faced on a regular basis had begun to take its toll.

Aaron cupped her shoulders. She'd never seen him look so serious before. "We just have to hang on a little longer. We'll figure this out…together."

She stared deep into his eyes and smiled. "We will."

It hurt to think about starting over, but she couldn't deny that she was attracted to Aaron. He was strong and courageous and handsome. Someone who would never let you down. Aaron was risking his life and his career for her.

"Thank you, Aaron. I can't imagine facing this without you. I'm so grateful," she said in earnest and his eyes softened as he looked at her and she lost herself in him for the moment.

"You're welcome," he said and kissed her forehead, then let her go. His smile faded and he stared at her with uncertainty.

Liz's heart slammed against her chest. Her gaze dropped to the ground, her emotions all over the board. He'd kissed her. Aaron had kissed her and she hadn't felt this way since… Eric. Was it too soon to have feelings for another man? Didn't Eric deserve more from her?

"Let's grab our gear and get out of here. Black Bear's still quite some distance away. I'd sure like to get there before dark if possible," he murmured and then moved away.

Aaron stowed their meager possessions in the snowmobile's compartment and turned to her. Liz tried to recover her composure but failed miserably.

"Ready?" he said and waited for her answer.

Slowly, she nodded. She was ready. So ready for this to be over.

Aaron got on, put on one of the helmets and then handed her the second one.

Once they were both on, he eased the machine from behind the office and onto one of the groomed paths.

Liz didn't understand Michael's full involvement with the weapons or their disappearance. The fact that he had accumulated evidence seemed to indicate that he had firsthand knowledge of the crimes committed to obtain them, but obviously the guns had been moved by someone she believed to be Michael. Something had changed his mind.

She still couldn't reconcile the possibility that Michael was in league with Sam. She knew Michael. He wasn't after money or obsessed with owning things. He was dedicated to protecting the country he loved.

"Why do you think he did it?" she asked because Aaron had known Michael almost as long as she had. They shared the common interests of hunting and fishing.

The length of time it took him to answer was revealing. "I don't know. Something was obviously wrong with him on the day he got out of the hospital, and there's no denying that he and Sam had a connection of some sort. I went over the videotape of Michael's visit. Their behavior was bizarre."

She drew in a breath and asked the question she needed to know. "And me? Do you think I'm guilty?"

Aaron didn't hesitate. "No. I never thought you were involved in Sam's crimes. You're too good a person. You've proven that to me countless times. We'll find out who's really behind this thing and the extent of Michael's involvement. And once we do, we can close the book on Sam and his deadly crimes once and for all. Then we can both look to the future…" He stopped as if he realized he'd said too much. She'd give just about anything to know the end of that sentence.

Aaron was a good man and he was risking everything to save her. Could she open her heart up to love again? It was too soon, surely? She couldn't just let Eric's memory go so easily.

She freed that thought for now. She was just so grateful to have Aaron on her side. He was the only thing keeping her going. Without his trust, she wasn't sure she'd care what happened to her.

The groomed path ended a little distance beyond the airstrip. Along the way, Aaron noticed several snowmobile tracks going in the same direction as them. Someone had been through here recently.

He'd kissed her. What had he been thinking?

He'd overstepped the line. He was her superior after all.

Still, he couldn't help it. Kissing her had felt right. He'd just gotten caught up in the moment and the way he felt about her. He couldn't deny that he had feelings for Liz that went beyond friendship, but he'd never intended to show them to her. She was still hurting over Eric's death. She wasn't ready. He wasn't even sure *he* was.

Aaron shook off his musings with difficulty. Something didn't feel right about the tracks he was seeing in the snow.

Michael had once told him that most of the hunting spots were some distance away from Black Bear, and yet the tracks seemed to be heading straight for the village.

Aaron feared he might have just lied to Liz. These tracks in addition to the information from the old man about other people in the area left Aaron with a bad feeling.

He spotted a sign indicating Black Bear was a couple of miles ahead and he stopped the snowmobile, removed his helmet, and got off. When Liz did the same he could see the worry on her face.

"What do you make of it?" she asked as his gaze followed the tracks leading into the village.

Aaron tried to remember any details Michael might have told him over the years about coming up here. He'd said the town was primitive in many ways. Most people who came here camped close to the river when fishing. Michael in fact had come to fish for salmon. He'd seemed to know a lot about it and Black Bear in general, which indicated he'd been here numerous times. Aaron didn't remember him ever mentioning hunting.

"There seems to be an awful lot of activity going on for it not being salmon spawning time," he said in answer to Liz's question. "To be safe, let's stash the snowmobile someplace protected and walk the rest of the way in."

She nodded and they scouted out a secure hiding spot.

Aaron did a quick search for the best place to leave the machine where it wouldn't be discovered. "Over there." He pointed to a thick patch of trees. "We can conceal it with branches for additional coverage." He'd guided the machine to the spot while Liz gathered branches to cover it and then covered their tracks.

They were both cold and damp and needed to get out of the elements as quickly as possible.

"It should be safe here unless someone ventures deeper into the woods," he told her. "Ready?"

She nodded and they started walking. Although it wasn't far from town, with the stress of the recent attacks, Aaron wasn't sure how much more Liz could take.

"It's not much farther," he tried to assure her.

She attempted a smile, but he could see she was

running on empty. She needed food and more important, rest. Neither seemed a possibility anytime soon.

They'd been walking for only a short amount of time when he heard it. The unmistakable sound of snowmobiles coming their way.

Liz froze. "They must be heading back to the airstrip."

"We need to get out of sight now." He pointed to some nearby trees. They barely had time to take cover before five machines came into view.

The machines were crawling along. Aaron held his breath. If the men noticed their footsteps they'd realize someone was out here besides them.

The last snowmobile passed them by when suddenly the vehicle in the lead braked.

"Hold up," the driver yelled and got off. Aaron peered through the trees and his pulse thundered against his chest. The man was looking at the ground.

He clutched Liz's shoulder and pointed. She saw what he did and her head whipped to him.

"We have to get out of here now," he mouthed and pointed in the direction of the village. They'd need to fight their way through the dense woods, but at least it was too thick for the snowmobiles to breach.

Aaron eased forward along with Liz.

"Someone's been here," the driver said.

"It's probably hunters," another man answered.

"One of the locals told me lots of people come here in search of moose. Besides, if it's the Scorpion agents, they wouldn't be on foot."

"Maybe, but we can't take any chances. We've lost touch with our men in Talkeetna and *he* should be here soon. We can't afford to look bad in his eyes again. You two, go back to the airport and see if the old man there knows of any new arrivals. Lean on him hard if you have to. The rest of you, come with me. We need to find out who these tracks belong to."

Aaron grabbed Liz's good hand and they ran as fast as they could. Behind them he could hear the snowmobiles firing and then slowly the sound faded. Voices could be heard in the woods nearby. They were heading their way.

"Hey, I see someone up ahead," one of the men yelled. "There are two people headed in the direction of Black Bear."

"We'll never make it to town before they reach us. We'll need to take them out," he said and looked to her for assurances she was up to the task.

Liz never wavered. "I can do my part."

"I'm going to backtrack a little so that I can take them by surprise. When they reach your location, start firing."

She understood. "Be careful, Aaron," she whispered.

He nodded. "I will. I'll see you soon," he said

with a confidence he didn't feel. The one thing that he and Liz had going for them was that they were trained in this type of fighting. He hoped it was enough to give them an edge.

Aaron had the Glock tucked behind his back and one of the assault rifles slung over his shoulder. He eased through the woods while listening carefully for anything out of the ordinary. A branch snapped nearby and he ducked quickly behind a tree. Drawing a deep breath, he glanced around and saw the three men moving through the woods. He tucked behind the tree once more until they were close to the area where Liz was hidden.

The second she opened fire, the two men in the lead froze, taken by surprise. The last man was a little ways behind. Aaron charged for him and wrapped his arm around his neck and choked him until he lost consciousness.

For the moment the men up ahead were unaware of their fallen comrade. They pinpointed the area where Liz had shot from and returned her fire. With a quick prayer for her safety, he raced for one of the men. Just as Aaron was right on top of him he turned. But it was too late. He hit him hard on the chin and the man dropped to the ground.

There wasn't much time. They needed to disable the last remaining person and get out of there before one of the unconscious men awoke.

The remaining man turned on Aaron with his weapon aimed at his heart.

"Whoa," Aaron said to throw the man off. Out of the corner of his eye, he spotted Liz as she charged the man. The man heard the noise and turned, but not in time to react.

With the last foe down, Aaron rushed to Liz's side. "We've got to keep moving. They'll be awake soon. We need to reach the village and get out of sight as quickly as possible because it won't take long before the men reach the airport and find out that we're here."

EIGHT

As they hurried through the trees at a fast pace, Liz struggled to keep from showing how exhausted she was.

Aaron stopped beside her and turned her to face him. She knew from the concern on his face that he was seeing what she hadn't wanted him to. "Hang in there," he said. "We're almost to Black Bear. Once we're out of sight, we'll get in touch with Jessie Chena. Hopefully, she can shed some light on what was going on with Michael."

Liz squared her shoulders. She wasn't a quitter. She had to keep pushing on for Michael and for Aaron.

"We're going to find out who this Safar person is and clear your name. With or without the evidence Michael gathered," he said with enough surety that she was inclined to believe him.

She smiled at him. "Yes, and when this is over, I owe you a home-cooked meal." She'd hoped to lighten the moment, only the warmth in his eyes as his gaze swept over her face took her breath away.

After a handful of seconds, he said, "We'd better get going." And she wondered if she'd said something to upset him or was it simply the urgency of the situation?

They'd gone only a few paces when the woods grew thinner and eventually disappeared and the small village of Black Bear came into view. Nothing about the narrow strip of a town was encouraging. There were but a handful of businesses, all of which appeared to have closed for the evening. Finding sufficient cover was going to be difficult.

Liz expelled a hopeless breath.

"Try Jessie's number," he urged. "We'll need her help."

She dug out the note from where she'd hid it in her boot and quickly called the number Michael had left for her. It went to voice mail—a woman's voice came on the recorder, identifying herself as real estate agent Jessie Chena. Liz didn't dare leave a message. Right now, she wasn't sure who to trust other than Aaron.

She ended the call. "It went to voice mail. But get this… Jessie Chena is a real estate agent. That's probably how she knows…knew Michael," she amended.

"No doubt it is." Aaron pointed to one of the faded wood structures that belonged to Black Bear Realty. "That must be her office. Let's use the cover of the building as protection against the wind."

Aaron quickly searched the area, but there didn't appear to be anyone around but them. They hurried to the side of the building where the roof's overhang provided some cover from the snowfall.

"Try her again," Aaron told her with renewed urgency. "I don't like being exposed like this. We need to get out of sight as soon as possible."

"The service is terrible," Liz said and unconsciously reached for his hand. When someone answered she said, "Hello, Jessie?" She immediately put the phone on speaker so that Aaron could hear the conversation.

"Yes, this is Jessie." After a pause filled with static, Jessie asked with an edge to her voice, "Who is this?"

Liz glanced up at Aaron who nodded. "Jessie, this is Liz Ramirez. I'm a friend of Michael Harris."

After a few tense seconds where Liz and Aaron stared at each other, the woman said, "I was beginning to think that Michael made you up. How can I help you?"

At least the woman recognized Liz's name, which gave some credence to Michael's story.

"Jessie, I'm in Black Bear and I need to talk to you right away. Can we meet tonight?"

The length of time it took the woman to answer didn't bode well in Aaron's mind.

"It's kind of late. My husband and I were just about to have dinner," the woman hesitated.

"I know and I'm sorry for the inconvenience, but it's important that I speak with you tonight. Can we come to you?"

Aaron could see that Liz didn't like the woman's reluctance to meet.

"No…wait, hang on," Jessie muttered and then they could hear noises in the background that sounded like a door closing. Then the woman returned to the call. "I can meet you at the Black Bear real estate office. I'm an agent there."

Liz frowned. "That's fine."

"I'll see you in thirty minutes." The woman disconnected the call without another word.

"That was strange," Aaron said. He hadn't liked the way the call had gone at all. "She's hiding something, but at least we have an idea on how they met. She could have sold him the cabin."

Liz shook her head. "Maybe, I guess so, but he never mentioned any of this to me." She rubbed her arms to stay warm.

"There's nothing open, otherwise we could get out of the cold. Maybe it's warmer close to the store entrance."

With an uneasy feeling in the pit of his stomach, they crept to the front of the building. There were only a handful of streetlights and none directly in front of the real estate office. They went up the steps to the porch. The windows had several available properties taped so that anyone passing by could see them.

"How did Michael ever find this place? It seems like a long way to travel just to go fishing."

Aaron could see she wasn't convinced. Not that he blamed her. It seemed odd to him as well.

"Black Bear is famous for catching salmon. Still, I remember when he talked about the village it was almost as if he had a personal connection to it somehow."

Liz shook her head as if she, too, was remembering it. "Let's hope some of our questions will be answered when we get to the cabin."

The quiet of the evening was broken by an engine's noise. It was coming their way. Immediately, Aaron was on alert. He peeked around the edge of the storefront. A snowmobile drew closer. Was it Jessie? He wasn't ready to take that chance just yet with so many armed men roaming around the area.

Aaron pointed to the opposite side of the building. "Let's wait there until we're sure this is Jessie."

Liz nodded and they hurried around to the side. Once they were out of sight, Aaron flattened himself against the side and peered around. The snowmobile drove past the building and then at the end of the road turned and went down the alley behind them. Once the driver reached the rear of their building, it stopped.

Aaron and Liz eased toward it for a closer look. A woman got off, hurried up the steps and unlocked the door.

"That must be her," Aaron said. They stayed in the shadows and followed the woman inside. She whipped around at the noise; her face looked terrified.

"Sorry, Jessie, it's me, Liz. We didn't mean to frighten you."

Jessie stared at them with real fear in her eyes while she struggled to control her emotions.

"This is Aaron," Liz turned to him at the introduction. "He's a good friend and you can trust him."

Still visibly shaken, Jessie said, "Sorry, I thought you might be…someone else."

Liz shot Aaron a look. "Who were you expecting?" she asked.

Jessie shook her head. "No one," she said in a noncommittal way and then moved a little away from them.

After a quick look around to make sure no one had followed Jessie, Aaron closed the door. The place was warm inside and he was grateful for the shelter.

"Come with me," Jessie told them in a nervous tone. "My office is through here and there's no windows. We can talk there."

She opened the door to what looked like a closet with a desk in it and turned on the lights. "Close the door. I can't stay long. I told my husband I would only be a little while and that I had a customer who wouldn't wait. He'll come looking for me if I don't get home soon."

"What are you afraid of, Jessie?" Liz asked and the look on the woman's face confirmed that she hadn't just been scared because she'd been surprised by their sudden appearance. There was more.

"I'm not afraid of anything," she answered in a sharp tone. "Why are you here? Where's Michael?"

Liz's gaze collided with Aaron's. He could see the warning in her eyes.

"He's not here, but he sent us to you," Aaron said. That was certainly true. They were here because of Michael.

"Is this about your cabin?" Jessie turned to Liz and asked, taking them both by surprise.

"My...cabin?" Liz asked, her eyes wide with astonishment.

Jessie glanced from her to Aaron. "Yes, the cabin Michael bought for you six months earlier. He said it would be a while before you came here to see it, but I was beginning to think something had gone wrong. I tried to reach him several times, but...has something happened?" Jessie asked in concern.

Liz finally overcame her shock. "I'm sorry, but I don't know what you're talking about."

Jessie slumped down into her chair. "You'd better sit down," she said and then heaved a heavy sigh. "I always thought it odd Michael would buy that particular cabin for someone else."

"What do you mean, *that particular cabin*?" Aaron asked.

Jessie hesitated, as if weighing how much to tell them, and Aaron's concern doubled.

"Michael said that you were a good friend and that he was helping you out. He said you were looking for a particular fishing cabin here in Black Bear. He paid cash for it. He told me when you showed up, you would finalize the paperwork." She glanced at Liz and added, "You didn't know about this, did you?"

Liz shook her head. "No, I had no idea." Aaron watched as she pulled out the map Michael had left her. "Did you give him this?"

Jessie recognized it right away. "Yes, that along with the key to the cabin."

"How far is it to where it's located? Can we get there tonight?" Liz asked.

Jessie shook her head. "There's no way you can make that trek in the dark. The terrain can be difficult even under the best of conditions. At night and with you both being unfamiliar, it could be deadly. Besides, you'll need a pretty rugged snowmobile to make it through the wilderness."

Aaron thought about the snowmobile they'd hidden in the woods. While it was adequate, there was no way it would cover the rugged terrain Jessie spoke of. They'd have to find another means of transportation.

"Look, I'm not sure what's going on here, but I urge you to wait until morning," Jessie counseled. "You can use my snowmobile. It'll get you there with no problem. If you'd like I could have my husband go with you. He knows the area well and he's a trained paramedic."

As much as Aaron would welcome traveling with someone with that kind of knowledge, they couldn't trust an outside party—it was already risky enough taking Jessie at her word.

"Why don't you two stay here tonight? It's not much, but it's warm and no one should bother you. This is our off season, so we're open by appointment only."

As much as he wanted to get to the cabin tonight and look for whatever Michael left there, Jessie was right. They'd be putting their lives in jeopardy by going there in the dark without knowing the area.

"She's right," Aaron said and could see Liz's disappointment. "We'll head out in the morning." He grabbed her good hand and gave it a quick squeeze. "We'll be okay."

Liz swallowed visibly and slowly smiled. "You're right. We will."

Jessie glanced at her watch. "I'd better go. My husband will be worried. Paul and I will bring the snowmobile by at first light," she said and Aaron smiled his appreciation.

"There's some food and drinks in the fridge in the office kitchen. It's not much, but help yourself to whatever you want," she said sympathetically. "Is there anything else I can help you with?"

Aaron shook his head. "No, we're grateful for the provisions and the use of your snowmobile tomorrow."

"It's no problem," she said genuinely and then added unexpectedly, "My house is one street over at the end of the block." She grabbed her business card and wrote down the address. "Just in case you need anything before the morning." With one final smile, Jessie walked out of the office.

Aaron would give anything to believe their ordeal was almost over, but he had a feeling it'd be a long time before they were no longer in danger.

NINE

Liz was going out of her mind with worry. So much was at stake. Her freedom. Aaron's career. The truth behind Michael's and Sam's deaths. *Their lives*.

Liz paced the tiny office with pent-up energy. She was exhausted down to her core and yet too keyed up to sit.

"Are you hungry?" She turned suddenly to Aaron after making her third trip around the office. The walls were closing in. She needed to be doing…something.

She thought about everything that was happening to them. Someone had carefully laid the groundwork to frame her, and then it seemed they'd anticipated every move she and Aaron made. She had never felt so helpless before. Her greatest fear now was that the evidence that could clear her name had been taken by the same people who were framing her.

"We could raid the fridge. Take our chances," she murmured.

Guilt tugged at her frayed emotions. Aaron appeared beyond exhausted. She attempted a smile for his sake and tried not to show the hopelessness growing inside her.

Yet when he came over to where she stood by the door and gently clasped her arms, it was obvious he saw through her attempt to hide her fear.

"We don't know if these people even realize the cabin exists," he told her in that quiet Southern way of his that seemed to always put things in perspective.

"We'll get a good night's sleep and start fresh in the morning. We're not done yet, Liz. Don't give up on me or on us."

As he looked deep in her eyes, she saw in them his unfaltering belief in her. She wouldn't give up on him ever—no matter what happened.

They might not know what they were facing or if they even would live through this, but suddenly all the things that she'd held on to that had prevented her from moving forward with her life were gone.

The last thing Eric would want her to do was spend the rest of her years grieving for him. And yet…the thought of opening her heart to another was a hard one.

As they continued watching each other, something shifted and Aaron's eyes darkened with the same emotion she imagined was reflected in her gaze.

Her heart beat a crazy rhythm against her chest. She'd felt this way before. With Eric. When they were...falling in love. She turned away and tried to tame her rapid heartbeat.

Liz faced him once more, ignoring the unasked questions in his eyes. "They shouldn't know the cabin exists, and their search wouldn't lead them there in any case since the paperwork hasn't been filed yet so there wouldn't be any record of me anywhere," she said in a less-than-steady voice.

As much as she'd tried to deny she had feelings that had moved beyond friendship for Aaron, the truth was staring her in the face in the breathless way she reacted to him every time she thought about his small kiss earlier that day.

The corner of his mouth lifted in a lopsided smile. "Exactly. And since it looks as if we'll be here the rest of the night, why don't we see what we can find to eat in the fridge? I just hope this time we have a better outcome. As I recall, the last time we had something to eat, we both ended up passed out and tied to a chair."

She could appreciate his joke now they were clear of that nightmare. At the time, well, it had been terrifying. She returned his smile and shoved aside any tender feelings. She was just so grateful to have him close. And it was nice to find something amusing after everything they'd been through.

They walked out of Jessie's office toward the tiny kitchen they'd seen earlier at the back of the building. It was next to impossible to see much more than her hand in front of her. "Do you think we can turn on some lights?" she asked while trying to calm her racing heartbeat.

Aaron pulled the blinds before turning on the lights. "Just to be safe, but we should be okay back here." He opened the door to the fridge and they both leaned in at the same time, their faces almost touching.

Just being close to him did dangerous things to her nerves. She'd almost forgotten what it felt like to have her pulse go crazy whenever someone was close.

"I see peanut butter and jelly. Maybe we can find some bread and have a PB and J?" Aaron said with a humorous wink.

She brushed back hair from her eyes. "I happen to love PB and Js. You'd be surprised how many times I end up having them. Cooking for one person is something I don't actually relish. More times than not, I put together something simple."

When she looked into his eyes, her chest grew tight once more with unexplored possibilities. Lately, when she needed to stay focused the most, she couldn't seem to get them out of her head.

As she watched, all of his former amusement left him. The look in his eyes made her wish for a different time. A different her. Where she could be free to give her heart to him.

Slowly they straightened and faced each other and she shuddered. He was going to kiss her and, oh, she wanted him to.

There was just enough time to second-guess the wisdom of the moment, before Aaron lowered his head and kissed her. Her heart drummed an excited beat while her head assured her it was too soon. She wasn't ready to go down that path again.

Her eyelids drifted closed. She didn't want him to see the chaos going on inside her. They'd shared so much together, worked through some difficult times in the past and he'd never once doubted her when everything pointed to her guilt. She... cared for him.

His lips were gentle against hers. Everything she believed his kiss would be. Filled with so much promise. She wanted to keep right on kissing him, forget about the trouble she was in for just a little while. Aaron was her safety net.

But a noise in the distance made her draw a shaky breath. As the sound grew louder and closer, Aaron ended the kiss and they stared at each other.

"What is that?" she whispered, her voice rough with emotion.

Aaron closed the fridge and she followed him

as he hurried to the front of the building where the sound had come from.

Once he'd cracked the blinds, she saw the headlights of at least three snowmobiles. They were cruising down the main street in front of their building. It was now pitch-black out. There would be no reason for anyone to be out at night.

"They're looking for something." He stated her thoughts aloud.

"Or someone…" Their gazes collided. "Aaron, it has to be the same men from earlier. They're looking for us."

"They're not going to give up until they find the weapons or they silence us."

He put his arm around her and drew her close to his side. "I'm not going to let that happen."

The vehicles made another pass through town before stopping at the end of the street. They killed their lights and engines.

"What do you think they're doing?" she asked fearfully.

"I don't know and I can't see anything from here."

She listened carefully and could hear multiple voices followed by what sounded like someone breaking down a door.

"They're searching the buildings. We can't stay here any longer. They'll be here before long." Adrenaline rushed through her veins. "What do you want to do?"

"There's only one choice. We won't make it back to the snowmobile and we can't afford to go wandering around in the subzero temperatures outside. Jessie said she lives on the next street over. We have to try to reach her house and she can give us shelter until morning. I just hope these guys don't intend to search the whole village."

Aaron cracked the door and listened closely before easing outside. Liz followed. Slowly they made their way toward the end of the street. Liz found herself constantly checking behind them.

Before they could cross the main street, several more snowmobiles came into view and she and Aaron tucked back into the shadows.

It seemed like the men just kept coming. "How many people are involved in this?" she asked in disbelief.

He glanced her way. "More than we know. The answers should be in the evidence Michael left behind. If they're not, or we can't find those files…" He didn't finish, but she knew exactly what he meant. They would have risked everything for nothing.

Liz saw the latest snowmobiles' headlights pull in close to the others. The men exchanged words, but she couldn't make out what they were saying.

She crept to the edge of the building where she could get a better view. "They're still on their vehicles. They don't seem to be joining in the search. We have to get off this street now."

Aaron glanced frantically around, looking for another way to cross. "Hang on. If we can make it just a little ways down from here, there's no streetlight." He pointed to the area. "We at least stand a chance of not being seen."

Keeping to the backs of the remaining buildings, they reached the place Aaron had indicated.

The men on the snowmobiles were still talking with their comrades. If they glanced their way, she and Aaron would be seen.

"We need to do it quickly. Are you ready?" Aaron asked.

When she didn't answer he clasped her hand, forcing her attention to him. "Liz?"

She wasn't anywhere close. She was exhausted down to her bones, but there was no other choice and she wasn't about to let Aaron down after everything he'd done for her.

She slowly nodded. "Yes, I'm ready," she whispered.

He smiled encouragement. "Good. Let's do this." Still holding her hand, they rushed out into the street and hurriedly crossed. Liz hadn't realized she was holding her breath until they'd reached the other side. Aaron pointed to the gap between two buildings.

They'd barely made it when something jumped out from the shadows. A dog, crouched low to the ground, snarled and edged menacingly closer blocking their way.

"We have to get past him and out of here. The noise is bound to draw their attention," Liz managed while keeping a careful eye on the dog.

Aaron dug into his pocket and pulled out a pen. "We need a distraction. Maybe we can get him to chase after it and buy us some time." He quickly tossed the pen down the alley in the direction he and Liz had come. The animal was obviously a stray. It rushed after the noise the pen had made, giving them the opportunity they needed to get away.

"Run and whatever you do, don't look back," Aaron said as she charged through the alley. She could hear his footsteps right behind her. And then snowmobiles firing up. The men had heard the dog's noise and were coming to investigate.

They barely had time to reach the end of the alley and round the corner before two machines screeched to a stop with their lights shining down the narrow passage. Liz ducked quickly to keep from being spotted.

The dog snarled at the men.

"Let's get out of here." One of them snapped. "There's nothing here but that mangy old mutt. I don't know where they are, but if those two agents are anywhere around this hole-in-the-wall town, we'll find them."

The men pulled the snowmobiles back out on the street and then left, the guy's parting words striking fear in her. They confirmed what she and Aaron both suspected.

"Aaron, they're not going to give up."

Every second they were out in the open like this, they risked capture.

Aaron stepped up on the porch and Liz followed. The temperature must have dropped twenty degrees since they'd arrived in town. They both were exhausted. They wouldn't survive long in this cold.

Please Lord, let them be home. He prayed silently because he didn't want Liz to see how worried he really was.

He knocked on the door and in the distance a dog barked in response to the sound.

As they waited, Liz glanced uneasily around and shivered. "I hope those men aren't listening for another dog," she said with an attempt at humor.

Aaron lifted a corner of his mouth in response. After a handful of seconds ticked by seeming more like an eternity, the door finally opened. Jessie stared at them for the longest time without being able to speak.

"Something's happened," she correctly assumed and then realized the chill out. "Come in where it's warm. You both must be freezing."

They went inside. After a quick look around outside Jessie closed the door.

"We're sorry to have to bother you again, but there's an awful lot of activity going on in town. It was no longer safe for us…" Aaron stopped when a man close to Jessie's age came into the room.

"It's okay—Paul knows everything. Please, come sit down. I'll make you something warm to drink to take away the chill."

Aaron watched Liz drop down into one of the kitchen chairs. From the way she held her wrist he knew it was hurting her. From where he stood, it looked as if it had swelled to twice its normal size.

"Let me take a look," he said gently. "You may have reinjured it."

She cradled it against her chest and nodded. "I think you may be right."

Aaron knelt in front of her. Their gazes holding for a second. As he slowly unwrapped the bandage, the pain on her face was hard to bear. He wished he could take it away. Make it better.

"The fracture looks worse than before," he said without mincing words.

"I'm a paramedic," Paul told them. "Let me examine it."

It didn't take long for Paul to reach the same conclusion as Aaron. "Your wrist is definitely reinjured," he diagnosed with a grim shake of his head. "I can give you something for the pain and I think I have a brace that will make you more comfortable, but you really need to see a doctor."

Liz shook her head. "That's not possible."

Paul slowly nodded. "Okay. I'll just go get the brace." He excused himself.

"You should stay here tonight." Jessie urged them with worry in her tone. "We have plenty of room and you both look ready to drop."

"That's a good idea and we're grateful," Aaron said with a weary smile.

Paul came back with some pain medicine and the brace. "I'll be as gentle as I can, but it's in pretty bad shape."

Liz swallowed a couple of the pills and nodded.

Aaron watched her clutch the table's edge with her good hand as Paul snugged the brace onto her wrist.

"That should keep it in place and hopefully help with the swelling. I've got some antibiotics that should stop it from getting infected."

"Thanks," Liz managed through clenched teeth. The effort had clearly taken its toll.

Jessie brought over two steaming bowls of chili and a couple of slices of cornbread. "You both need to eat. It's not much, but it will give you some energy."

Aaron took the seat next to Liz and tasted a spoonful of the spicy chili. "It's wonderful, Jessie," he said and then dug into the food with relish.

"I'm glad you like it," Jessie said and she and her husband joined them. "Why are these men following you anyway? They've been in town most of the day. Someone said they were here for the hunting, but they don't much look like hunters, if you ask me."

Aaron could almost feel Liz's anxiety growing from where he was. He understood it all too well. They weren't sure who to trust. Even people as innocent looking as Jessie and Paul could be working for the enemy.

He decided for their own safety not to divulge too many details. "We believe they're looking for something Michael might have brought here. He didn't ask you to store anything for him recently, did he?"

Jessie was obviously confused by the question. "No, but then, I haven't spoken to him in months. Not since he bought the cabin for you."

If Michael hadn't contacted Jessie to store the weapons, then where were they?

"Do you remember much of what you talked about that last time you spoke to him?" Aaron asked. He knew it was a long shot, and he was clutching at straws, but he was desperate. Those men were not going away.

"We really didn't talk that much. I thought it was strange that he paid cash for the cabin, though. I've never had a customer do that before."

"Did Michael mention what he did for a living that would allow him to have so much cash on hand?" Liz asked curiously.

"Only that he'd left the Marines and that the

money, well, he said that was from you. He told me you gave it to him and asked him to buy the cabin for you." Jessie hesitated. "Is Michael okay?" she asked the question Aaron had known was coming.

He glanced at Liz who nodded. "I'm sorry to have to tell you this, Jessie, but Michael's dead. He was murdered."

It was a long time before Jessie answered. "I can't believe it. Who would want to kill Michael?" she said in a trembling voice as tears filled her eyes.

"That's what we're trying to find out," he told her. Aaron thought about the funds that had gone into Liz's account recently. Someone had gone to great lengths to make sure she looked guilty. He didn't like it. Every second they were unable to reach the cabin, they risked the chance of the enemy finding the place and the evidence and destroying Liz's last hope to clear her name.

Another far more disturbing thought had him wondering if Michael had been the one to set her up all along.

The noise of engines drawing closer pulled his attention back to the moment. They sounded just outside the Chenas' home.

Liz gripped his arm. "They must be going house to house," she whispered in a frantic voice.

Jessie's eyes grew wide. "What should we do?"

Whether or not the men discovered them depended on Jessie and Paul not giving anything away.

"Just try to act normal," Aaron told her. "If they ask if you've seen us today, tell them no. You've been home all evening and you haven't seen a thing, okay?"

Jessie managed a minuscule nod.

"It's going to be okay," Aaron tried to assure her but he was worried. "Liz and I will be in the next room if something goes wrong."

A deafening knock at the door had Jessie jumping to her feet. She covered her mouth as if to keep from screaming.

Liz cast an uneasy look his way. Jessie was vulnerable. If pressed she wouldn't be able to keep with the story.

"Let me answer it, Jess," Paul said and squeezed her shoulder then gave her a gentle nudge toward the kitchen. "You pretend you're making dinner."

Not wanting to give away the truth to anyone looking too closely, he saw Jessie hurriedly hide their bowls and Paul's medical bag, then grab a wooden spoon and stir the chili.

Liz hurried into the living room and he followed. Making sure to keep away from the windows, they drew their Glocks to be on the ready. The assault rifles they'd brought with them from Rick's place were within arm's reach as they leaned against the wall closest to the kitchen.

Liz drew in a breath. Aaron wished he could reassure her everything was going to work out okay, but he wasn't anywhere close to being convinced it would.

Another angry knock rattled the walls. A moment later, Paul opened the door.

"Can I help you two gentlemen?" Paul asked, whether deliberately or not giving Aaron and Liz some information on how many were at the door.

"Yes, you can. Tell me who's been at your house tonight?" One of the men tried to disguise the command as a friendly question.

Paul didn't hesitate. "There's no one here but my wife and I and we're about to have dinner. What's this about?" he asked, seamlessly pulling off the deception.

The same man answered. "We're bounty hunters searching for some people. A man and a woman who we believe are here in Black Bear. And there are footprints leading from the alley up to your house. Are you sure you haven't seen anyone?" The accusation in his tone was clear.

"Hum, well I'll be, they sure do. Maybe they kept moving." Paul must have stepped out on the porch. "All I know is no one's been here tonight and if they're out there in these temperatures, you won't have to worry about bringing them in. They'll be dead by morning."

The man made a noncommittal *harrumph* noise. "And how do I know you're telling the truth?" He voiced his doubts. "You could be hiding them."

Aaron heard the door creak open and he held his breath. Would Paul give them up?

"As you can see, there's no one here but my wife. Now, if you don't mind, we're about to settle in for the night."

The other man said something unintelligible and then the door closed. Seconds slipped by before the engines fired and the vehicles moved away.

Paul came into the living room. "I think they've left for now, but they definitely know about you two and I'm not sure he bought my story completely."

Aaron tucked his Glock behind his back. "Thank you. I'm sorry to have gotten you and Jessie involved in this, but there wasn't any other option."

Paul shook his head. "It's no problem. Obviously, those men are up to no good and I don't believe their story about being bounty hunters one little bit. Still, come daylight, they'll widen the search. You two need to get out of town before that happens."

Aaron's sleep-deprived mind tried to come up with an escape plan.

"I know Jessie promised we'd stop by the office with our extra snowmobile. The offer still stands," Paul said. "I'll drive Jessie to work tomorrow. With all this going on, I think I'll stay as close to her as possible."

"Thank you," Aaron said, humbled by the man's generosity. "It's probably a good idea to stay close to Jessie. We don't know what these guys are capable of if they figure out you've helped us."

"Are you federal agents?" Jessie asked growing more suspicious of them.

"Yes, we are," Aaron told her quietly. "We're trying to figure out how Michael is connected to these men."

Jessie looked to her husband who nodded and Aaron could tell there was something she needed to tell them.

"What is it?" he asked curiously.

"I didn't say anything before because, well, I didn't really trust you, and for that I'm sorry."

Aaron glanced at Liz. She had braced herself for what was to come next.

"Michael and I dated for a while in high school," Jessie blurted out.

This was the last thing he expected. "Michael was from Black Bear?" Aaron asked while his exhausted brain tried to make sense of it. He looked to Liz for answers.

She shook her head. "I had no idea Michael had lived here before. The only place he mentioned from his past was somewhere in Montana," she told him.

Jessie slowly nodded. "He did live in Montana

when he was a kid. You see, Michael's family was part of an Amish community that came to Alaska to set up a colony here, only it didn't work out. Michael's mother returned to Montana and rejoined their community there, but Michael and his father, well, they left their faith. Michael lived in Black Bear from about the time he was twelve until he graduated from high school."

"That's how you met him," Aaron concluded.

They'd been right. Michael's relationship with Jessie seemed awfully close for a business arrangement.

Jessie glanced briefly at her husband and then nodded. "Yes, my family moved to Black Bear when I was a freshman in high school. I met Michael then. We were…high school sweethearts. He was so dear back then." She shook her head.

"Once he left town, I didn't see him for a long time. Then he showed up again and, well, he was so different. Withdrawn. Suspicious. Like another person completely."

"When was this?" Liz asked, puzzled.

"A couple of years ago."

She and Aaron stared at each other in shock. Had Michael been in Sam's pocket for so long?

"Michael wasn't even part of the Scorpions back then," Aaron said.

He could see that Liz had remembered something important. "What is it?" he asked.

"I remember something Michael mentioned

once about how determined he'd been to join the team." She hesitated. "He said he was willing to do just about anything."

The implication was alarming. Had Michael deliberately targeted the Scorpions so that he could assist Sam with his plans?

"Have you spoken to Michael's brother yet?" Jessie asked, the question taking them both by surprise.

"Wait—Michael has a brother?" Liz said in disbelief.

Jessie seemed surprised that they didn't know. "Oh, yes. Although from what Michael told me, he was quite a bit older."

"Do you know how we can reach him?" Aaron asked while trying not to get too excited. It could be another lie, but if there was a brother who lived close by, maybe he'd be able to shed some light on what happened to Michael.

Jessie shook her head. "No, I'm sorry, I don't even remember his name although I'm sure Michael must have mentioned it a couple of times."

Aaron watched as what little bit of hope he'd seen in Liz evaporated. They were back to square one.

"I'm sorry. I wish I could help you more," Jessie said, obviously seeing their disappointment.

Aaron attempted a smile. "We'll figure this out and we're grateful for all that you two have done for us."

Liz stifled a yawn. She looked ready to drop.

"You should get some sleep," he told her gently. "Tomorrow's going to be a difficult day." They'd need to be gone before daybreak. "Can I see the map on the note Michael gave?"

She didn't hesitate. "Sure," she told him and retrieved it from her boot and handed it to him.

He studied the map. It showed the cabin, but he needed more information on the landscape. "Is this the best way to reach the cabin?"

"Hang on a second," Paul said and took out a more detailed map of the area and spread it out on the table. "The place gets lots of snow, but it should still be accessible by snowmobile…although it won't be easy." He pointed out the best route. It wound through the wilderness for several miles then climbed upward until it reached the base of Black Bear Mountain where the structure was located.

Just looking at the path they'd have to take was discouraging.

Liz touched his hand, seeing his despair. "We'll get through this together."

He looked at her lovely face and realized she was counting on him. He couldn't let her down.

"We'll clear out of here pretty early," he told Paul. "We don't want to put you and Jessie in any more danger than we have already."

"The machine you should use is the black one in the garage," Paul told them. "The key's in it.

It's fueled and there's an extra gas can strapped on the back."

"Thanks," Aaron said with a shake of his head.

"The extra bedroom is through there," Jessie pointed to a door. "And there's a bathroom's down the hall. I'll just get you some sheets for the sofa," she told Aaron and left them alone.

Aaron stepped closer. He could see Liz was fighting back tears. "It's going to be okay," he said softly so that only she could hear.

She looked deep into his eyes. She was vulnerable and beautiful and he was so attracted to her.

Something of the battle raging inside him must have shown on his face because she asked, "Are you okay?"

He closed his eyes briefly and then nodded and turned away.

"Thank you for believing in me, Aaron," she whispered.

He turned to face her. She looked like a lost child pleading her cause and he stroked his cheek. He wished for a happy ending to this for her.

"I'd do anything for you. Anything at all." He leaned close and touched his lips to hers. "Get some sleep. You'll feel better in the morning."

He stepped away and after a second she left him. He had to believe that what they were going through was only for the moment. With God's help, they'd unravel the truth.

TEN

Aaron had barely managed a couple of hours' sleep during the long night. His mind wouldn't shut down. He kept listening to the noises outside. Hearing snowmobiles everywhere. He was worried about Liz's injuries. And if they'd even find anything useful at the cabin when they finally got there. But mostly, he was troubled about his unexpected reaction to Liz.

She wasn't Beth—he knew this. Nothing about her reminded him of Beth, and yet the fallout from Beth's deception had left him one of the walking wounded. Unable to trust. He couldn't put himself in that situation again. Still, Liz's strength showed during the toughest times, the way she laughed at his attempts to be funny, the way she felt in his arms, had him rethinking his hard-and-fast rule about never falling in love.

A sound close by caught his attention, changing the direction of his thoughts and putting him on high alert. He grabbed his gun.

Paul stopped dead in his tracks when he spotted the Glock. "Whoa…sorry, man, I was just about to wake you."

Aaron blew out a relieved-sounding breath and got to his feet. "No, it's okay. To say I'm a little on edge is putting it mildly." He waited a few seconds for his heart to stop pounding and said, "You didn't have to get up so early." He glanced at the darkness beyond the blinds. "What time is it anyway?"

"Just past five. You have about another hour before daybreak. I thought I'd make you both some coffee and food for the trip." Paul hesitated. "Are you sure you're up to it? Your friend is in pretty bad shape."

The warning coming from someone in the medical profession didn't ease his bad feeling one little bit.

"I'm afraid we don't have a choice. There's something at the cabin we need and we have to find it before those men do."

Paul accepted the answer without questioning it. "I'll give you some medicine to take with you. Cell service is pretty much nonexistent on good days, especially up in the high country. Still, if you can find a clearing you may be able to make a call."

He handed Aaron a slip of paper. "That's my number. I'm part of a search and rescue team that works the area. I know that trail like the back of my hand. Wherever you are, I'll find you." He paused and then added, "I could go with you, if you'd like."

As tempting as it sounded, Aaron couldn't put Paul's life in jeopardy like that.

"Thanks, but I can't ask you to do that. There's too much at stake. We'll be fine," Aaron tried to assure him without really believing it himself.

Paul poured hot coffee into a couple of thermoses. "Okay, but I'm serious. If you need assistance, call me."

Aaron smiled. "I will. Thanks for the help and the food."

A door opened and Liz came into the kitchen. She looked much better after a good night's sleep.

"How are you feeling?" he asked because they had a rough day ahead of them and he needed to know she was up to it.

"Much better." She held up her wrist. "The brace helped tremendously."

"We should be on our way while it's still dark out," Aaron told her.

Jessie stood in the doorway. "Not until you have breakfast. You two need something warm inside you for the ride."

Aaron shook his head. "Thanks, Jessie, but there's no time. We need to get out of here before those men come back."

Jessie clearly didn't like his answer, but she understood. "Okay, but at least let me make you some sandwiches for the road. I'll pack some extra food and water as well."

Jessie quickly put together some sandwiches and supplies for the journey and put them in Liz's backpack. "You'll need some warmer jackets too. Paul and I have extra. I'll get them for you."

Aaron took the backpack full of supplies and he and Paul went out to the garage.

"I'll wait to open the door until you're ready to leave, in case someone's watching. The trail begins just behind our house. Head straight for the woods. Some of the town folk still hunt in those woods, so the trail should be groomed for a little ways in. Once you start to ascend the mountain, you may be in for some deep snowdrifts, though."

Paul went over to a workbench and brought back a shovel and some snowshoes. "This will help. There are more tools in the side pouch. As I said, cell service is sketchy at best. I never leave the house without being prepared. The cabin's about ten miles up the trail, to your left, at the base of the mountain. It's the only one in that area. You won't miss it."

"Are there other cabins around?" Aaron asked curiously. If the place was isolated, the chances of someone just happening on it were slim. There might still be a chance the evidence was still untouched.

Paul shook his head. "Not really. There are a few hunting cabins, but no one lives in them.

They're used by hunters and trappers from time to time or if someone gets caught out in the weather. There's usually some supplies kept in them, but it's minimal."

When Liz came into the garage, Aaron noticed that she had donned a heavy winter parka, cap and gloves. Jessie handed him a second parka and gloves.

"I'll help you get the machine out," Paul said and opened the garage door.

With his breath coming quickly, Aaron eased outside and surveyed the surrounding area. The house was at the end of the street. There was no sign of the men from the previous evening, still, he didn't doubt for a minute that they'd be broadening their search at first light.

The trail behind the house looked tame compared to what he knew they'd face once they started the climb. With Paul's help, he got the machine from the garage and pointed toward the direction they'd be taking.

"Thanks again for all your help," Aaron said with indebtedness and clasped Paul's hand.

"You're welcome, but please be careful. There can be much more danger in those woods than just the men chasing you." The warning settled uneasily around Aaron. He had no doubt there were things in the woods that would be more than he and Liz could handle.

"You'll let us know what's truly going on here,

won't you?" Jessie asked in a whisper of a voice. "I would really like to understand what happened to Michael."

"We will. I promise," Aaron smiled and assured them.

Once they'd said their goodbyes, Liz got on the machine behind him. Although she looked much better, the rugged Alaskan terrain was going to take its toll on both of them and he was anxious to be on the way.

Aaron slowly guided the snowmobile down the path. The quiet of predawn was shattered by its sound. He just hoped most people wouldn't think twice about hearing a snowmobile in town, even at this hour of the morning.

Liz wrapped her arms around his waist.

"Aaron, do you think this Safar person is the one Sam double-crossed?" she asked.

He'd wondered the same thing. In his mind there was only one answer.

"I believe so. Something must have went south between them, though." He had no idea what.

"If what Rick said was correct and the weapons never reached Talkeetna, did they somehow get diverted here? It doesn't make sense. The men said they searched Black Bear and what I'm assuming was the place where they were supposed to take the delivery. They weren't there." The wind snatched at her words so that he barely heard them.

Nothing about bringing the guns to Black Bear made sense. It seemed like a risky passage in the first place. He had a feeling Michael had somehow moved them to an entirely different location.

Aaron kept remembering the odd exchange between Michael and Sam. They had both acted as if they were angry with each other.

"After everything that happened, there's no doubt in my mind that Michael somehow managed to double-cross Sam and move the weapons somewhere else. I'm guessing he had second thoughts about handing them over to the buyer," Aaron said.

Whoever this Safar was, and whatever his plans were, Michael must have realized the consequences of turning them over to him.

"And if the final destination was Black Bear, then they would have to have people along the way helping out and certainly someone here to receive the cargo and get it out of sight quickly," he added. "I don't think the weapons ever made it here."

"I agree," Liz said with a sigh. "Let's just hope the evidence Michael left at the cabin is still there and it's enough to fill in all the holes in our theory because right now, we don't know Safar's real identity. And we need more to go on than a single name."

The predawn twilight quickly turned black once they entered the dense forest. The temperature had to be well below zero and it was snowing again, reducing Aaron's visibility greatly. He had to continually wipe his visor off just to see where he was going. One false move and the snowmobile would be buried. They couldn't afford to lose time digging it out.

They'd need to get to the cabin as soon as possible and out of sight. He knew the men who had followed them to the Chenas' home the evening before weren't going to give up until they had them. Dead or alive.

"I just hope they don't know about the cabin…" Liz said and then stopped as if something had occurred to her. "Aaron, what if we're wrong and Michael moved the weapons to the cabin? Maybe that's the evidence he spoke of in the note? It's certainly remote enough that no one would deliberately look for them there."

Notwithstanding the difficulty of getting that much weaponry to such an isolated location, Liz was right about one thing: it would be the perfect hideaway.

But the cabin was intended for Liz, according to Jessie. He didn't voice his concerns aloud, but if they did find the weapons, Michael having supposedly bought the cabin for her would certainly make her look suspicious. He pressed her hand. "We'll figure it out. God didn't bring us all this way without a reason. We'll find what we need to clear your name and once we locate the weapons, we'll bring the real killer to justice. Don't give up."

She hugged him tight and he tried to let go of his misgivings, but it was a near-impossible feat.

The farther in the woods they traveled, the deeper the snow piled up. The lack of sunshine meant there was no snowmelt.

"What I don't understand is how Michael came up with the money to buy the place. How long has he been working for Sam?" Aaron voiced his concerns. "To get enough money to pay cash without calling attention to himself tells me he was on Sam's payroll for a while. You knew him better than any of us. He never mentioned anything?" He hated the doubt in his tone, but Liz and Michael were close. Maybe there was something she'd overlooked telling him without even realizing it.

He knew he'd hurt her with his question when she didn't answer right away. "He never mentioned anything that made me suspicious. Don't you think I'd tell you if he had?" she finally said with hurt in her voice.

"I don't think you're involved, Liz." He did his best to assure her—and himself—against the doubts that were crowding in. "I'm just thinking that maybe he mentioned something you forgot or dismissed as unimportant. We don't know what we'll face once we get to the cabin. It would help to have some clue."

She blew out a heartfelt breath. "You're right and I'm sorry. I'm just so ready for this to be over."

"I know. Me too," he told her and meant it.

She'd been through so much. It was time for something good to happen to make up for the bad.

Up ahead, Aaron noticed that the groomed trail came to an abrupt halt. He braked hard. No one had traveled beyond this point recently, which was a good sign the enemy wouldn't be waiting for them once they reached their destination. But the roughened path also meant he'd have to push the machine to its max.

"Is it safe to go on?" Liz asked uneasily after seeing the difficulty.

"I don't think we have a choice. We can make it, but it's going to slow our time down by a lot." Aaron slipped off his helmet and listened carefully. In the distance he could hear the vigorous roar of multiple engines coming from the direction of town. Was it the men they'd seen the day before or just normal everyday life in Black Bear?

"Are you ready?" he asked Liz. After a doubtful second she nodded. "Hang on as tight as you can. We're going to be traveling at full speed."

He shoved the machine into high gear and they headed for the ungroomed stretch of woods, slugging through the thick snow accumulated there. Several times the machine came close to stalling out, yet Aaron dared not push it any harder.

They'd gone a little ways farther into the forest when a far more alarming sound captured his attention. A chopper—and it was gaining!

"Where is it?" Liz asked, having heard the

same thing. Before he had time to answer, it appeared over the trees and right above them.

In Aaron's mind, there was no doubt. "They're searching for us." He did his best to avoid the chopper's spotlight as it came within inches of the snowmobile. Steam rose from the motor. "We have to stop. The engine's getting hot." He glanced around for a place to hide as the spotlight continued searching the ground near them. It came close to finding them several times.

"Over there." Liz pointed to their right. "There's a partially-downed tree. We can use it as camouflage."

Aaron eased the snowmobile in that direction while keeping a careful eye above them.

Once he'd stopped, he turned off the machine. Heat rose in the air emphasizing the strain the engine had been under.

Overhead, the chopper continued its methodical search.

"There's no way they know it's us," Aaron told her. "And they can't randomly fire on us without knowing who they're shooting at." He said a silent prayer in his head that he hadn't lied. These people had already proven themselves ruthless. What were a few more bodies?

The chopper's pilot lowered the machine as much as it dared.

Liz's arms tightened around him. "Aaron, they've spotted us."

"We don't have a choice. We have to use the snowmobile to get out of here." He fired the engine. "Hold on. We're going to have to make a run for it. Let's just hope it holds together long enough for us to escape."

Soon they were under attack. Bullets were flying from a semiautomatic weapon being fired by one of the men above them. Aaron somehow managed to keep the overheated machine going as he attempted to save their lives.

The pilot wasn't letting up. He followed their movements with the spotlight.

"They're still coming," Liz yelled over the noises around them.

She knew that Aaron was doing his best to lose them in the thick woods while avoiding the thick growth of trees.

"Whatever we do, we can't lead them to the cabin." Liz warned. "I'm going to try something," she told him.

While Aaron headed in the opposite direction of the cabin, falling back on her training as a sniper, Liz pulled out one of the assault rifles she'd taken from the men at Talkeetna and aimed for the spotlight. With the jostling of the snowmobile, it took two tries before she hit the target and the light exploded.

"Nice job," Aaron said in what sounded like awe. "That should give us a chance at least, but they'll still be able to see us with our headlights on and I can't afford to drive this thing without them. I don't know the terrain here."

They were quickly running out of time and options.

"If we can make it to the base of the mountain, the chopper won't be able to get too close. It would risk slamming into the mountain. I have an idea. I need your help," he told her.

"Anything. Just name it." She was quick to assure him.

"I'm going to draw them out of the tree coverage. When we're clear and you have a clean shot, take out their engine."

His confidence in her sharpshooting ability was obvious.

As Aaron kept the machine as steady as possible, Liz aimed the rifle.

One of the men on board leaned out of the chopper and fired, striking the snowmobile's cooling system. The already overheated engine spewed coolant and Aaron was forced to stop.

Liz fired several rounds into the chopper's engine. Smoke billowed and the chopper dipped and dove toward the ground before the pilot managed to right it and turn around heading in the direction of the town.

"I don't think I destroyed it, but at least it's limping," she told him.

"Good job. You bought us some time." Aaron

got off the machine and examined the engine. "Unfortunately, we're not going anywhere on this thing."

She glanced around the desolate area. "We can't stay here for long. They'll be back soon enough."

Liz took out her cell phone and tried it, then shook her head.

"We should get going," Aaron said. At least there's a couple of sets of snowshoes in the supplies Paul gave us. That'll help us to maneuver and if the snow continues to fall that should cover our tracks."

She took the snowshoes Aaron handed her and secured them on her feet, then slung one of the assault rifles over her shoulder while Aaron strapped on her backpack filled with supplies and took the second weapon.

"We need something to help us walk in this deep snow," she said after only a few steps. Even with the snowshoes, maneuvering through the piles of snow would be exhausting at best. Liz searched the area until she found some downed tree limbs that could serve as walking sticks.

Aaron smiled at her. "Good idea." He took out the map Paul had given them. "According to these directions, the cabin's a good five-mile trek that way." He pointed to the left. "At least it's mostly downhill. That's something, I guess." She could tell he was trying to remain positive.

She'd do her best as well. They had a long hike

ahead of them and her injured wrist was hurting like crazy, but Liz was determined not to let him see the pain.

"We should head out..."

Slugging through several feet of snow, with each step causing them to sink into the white slush, was an exhausting task. After barely a quarter of a mile they were both breathing hard and were forced to stop to catch their breath.

"How are you holding up?" Aaron asked and handed her a bottled water.

She nodded to conserve her breath. She was sweating from the exertion and worried about exposure, and the ache in her wrist had increased tenfold.

"Here, take one of the pills Paul gave you. It will help with the pain."

"Thanks," she said and took the pill from him and swallowed it.

Once they started walking again, a sobering thought occurred to her.

"Aaron, what happens when we reach the cabin? Even if we find the evidence Michael left, depending on what it is, how are we going to get it back to the plane? Especially if there's no phone service and these men are closing in."

He shook his head. "We'll figure it out once we get there. Let's just get out of the open."

Soon enough the woods disappeared and they could see the base of the mountain rising in the early morning above a thick fog. The snow hadn't let up and the temperature continued to drop.

Aaron glanced up at the sky. "We'll never make it like this. We need someplace to get out of the weather. Hopefully, the storm will pass soon."

Liz looked around them anxiously for something to provide shelter. Then she remembered something Jessie's husband had said. "Didn't Paul say there are several hunter cabins around the area?"

"Yes, he did." Aaron pulled out the map that Paul had given him. She could see where Paul had marked the cabins' locations. "There's one off to the right about a quarter of a mile from here. Unfortunately, it's the opposite direction of where we need to be, but still, it's closer and at least we can get inside."

The wind howled with renewed anger as the storm's ferocity increased. The conditions were worsening by the minute and Aaron grabbed Liz's good hand to keep her from toppling over several times.

They'd almost reached the hunting cabin when she heard what sounded like a twig breaking close by and she jerked around. Through the driving snow, nothing could be seen. She tapped Aaron's arm and he turned.

"I thought I heard something behind us," she whispered in his ear.

He peered through the whiteout. "I don't see anything. Maybe it was just an animal."

She didn't believe it for a second.

Aaron pointed up ahead. "There's the cabin." His relief was obvious. They hurried toward it.

Once they reached the front of the place, Aaron stopped her. He drew his weapon and she did the same. Liz couldn't shake the eerie feeling they were being watched. Was the threat real or were they just paranoid due to what they'd gone through?

Slowly, Aaron opened the door and they rushed inside with weapons drawn. The cabin consisted of a single room with a wood stove in the corner. There were a couple of chairs pulled up next to it.

"At least it's warmer in here," he said and lowered his weapon.

"I'm grateful for the chance to sit for a while." Liz dropped down to one of the dusty chairs and closed her eyes.

"Me too."

But when she opened her eyes once more Liz realized Aaron hadn't done the same. Instead, he was over by the window glancing out.

All of a sudden she saw him move quickly and tuck himself behind the door. She immediately jumped to her feet.

"What is it?" she asked, but believed she knew the answer. It hadn't just been her imagination. There had been someone behind them.

ELEVEN

"You were right. Someone is back there," he told her, unable to hide his concern.

Keeping low, Liz crept over to where he stood. "How many?"

"I only saw one man." Aaron pointed in the direction they'd come. "He was looking straight at the cabin and not trying to disguise his presence. I don't like it."

"What do you want to do?" she asked while searching the tree line. "I see him."

If this guy was part of the team of men that had been chasing them, then why wasn't he being more discreet? "Why is he out here alone?" In Aaron's mind it didn't make sense that one of Safar's goons would be there by himself.

She shook her head. "None of the men following us were traveling on their own. Maybe he is simply a hunter."

Paul had told them that the cabins were used by hunters.

As they watched, the man slowly headed for the house. He had a weapon slung over one shoulder. Still, the possibility of him being out in the middle of nowhere was just too big of a coincidence for Aaron to ignore.

"Stay here and cover me. I'm going to see what he wants."

"Aaron, be careful. We don't know who this guy is."

"Don't worry." He managed a smile for her. "If he tries anything, shoot first. We can question him after he's subdued."

Aaron stepped outside, aware of Liz opening the single window. She would be ready if the man did something suspicious.

The man was dressed in a heavy camo. His head covered with a fur hat.

"That's far enough," Aaron said when the man was within striking distance. "Why are you following us?"

The man smiled at Aaron's stern greeting. It occurred to him that the stranger didn't appear surprised to see him. Had he been watching them?

After a few seconds the man said, "I'm not following you. I was trapping in the area and I heard an exchange of gunfire from my camp. I was worried. Are you and your partner okay?"

It stood to reason that he'd heard the firefight. Anyone within a ten-mile radius would have heard it. Still, Aaron couldn't let it go.

The guy tentatively stepped closer and introduced himself. "My name's Davis Kincaid. I used to live around here and I still come up every year at this time to trap."

The man held out his hand. After a moment's hesitation, Aaron took it. "Aaron Foster. How'd you get out here anyways, Davis?" he asked not bothering to hide his suspicions.

Davis's smile didn't falter. "I hiked in from town a few weeks back. I've been camping around the area, running trap lines ever since."

"Had any success?" Aaron asked, keeping him engaged long enough to get a good read off the man.

Davis's laughter seemed genuine enough. "I'm afraid I'm a bit rusty. I've seen plenty of tracks, but so far, I haven't managed to catch a single fur."

Aaron didn't get the feel Davis was involved with the people who'd been coming after them, but still, he believed Davis's intentions were questionable.

"I just wanted to know if there was anything I could do to help."

Aaron wasn't about to open that door. "No, we'll be okay. We're going to rest for a bit and then move on."

"You have a destination in mind?" The question came out a little too sharp for Aaron's taste. "I know the area pretty well. I could help you get there," Davis amended.

"Not really. We're just hunting ourselves. I think the people in the chopper must have thought we were prey."

Davis nodded, but Aaron could see he didn't believe him. It was as if they were playing a cat-and-mouse game with each other, dealing in half-truths.

"You sure I can't help?" Davis pressed.

Aaron shook his head. "No, we're good. Hope the trapping goes well."

"You too," Davis said and turned and headed back in the direction he came.

Before Aaron had managed more than a single step back toward the cabin, he heard in the distance what sounded like multiple engines roaring through the woods. Out of the corner of his eye he caught Liz racing from the cabin. Three sets of headlights bounced off the trees heading their way.

"The chopper must have radioed our coordinates to them," Aaron told her grimly.

Davis hurried back to them. "What's going on here? Who's on those snowmobiles?" he asked and Aaron debated how much to tell him. "Are they connected to the people who were chasing you in the chopper?"

"I'm not sure," Aaron told him. His misgivings over Davis's sudden appearance doubled. Why was the man out here alone? Aaron didn't buy his story about being a trapper for a second.

"What do they want with you two?" Davis pressed in a hard tone while Aaron's gaze locked with Liz's. He could see the warning in her eyes. She didn't trust Davis either.

It was pretty convenient that the man just happened to appear out of the woods seconds after the attack.

Still, while he wasn't sure of Davis's intentions, the snowmobiles were gaining on them quickly. They couldn't stay out in the open like this.

"Look, if we stay here much longer, we're sitting ducks. We have a better odds at holding them off from inside. So you can either come with us, or take your chances with them," Aaron said and motioned toward the noise.

"Let's go before they spot us," Liz told them both.

Davis stared at them for a second longer, then turned on his heel and headed for the cabin, clearly not satisfied with Aaron's answers.

"I don't trust him," Aaron told her once Davis was out of earshot.

Liz nodded. "I don't either. We need to keep our guard up," She pulled something from her pocket. "I have extra clips for the assault rifles." She handed him some of the ammo. This should help us fight them off for a while. Who knows how many more they'll send if these guys aren't successful."

He could see the fear in her eyes she couldn't

hide and he gently touched her face. "Hey, we're not defeated yet."

She smiled. He was trying so hard to keep from showing her how desperate their situation was and yet she knew. "No, we're not."

"Come on, we'd better hurry out of sight before they get here."

"Unfortunately, there's no hiding our tracks," Davis told them once they entered the cabin. "They'll know someone's here. I doubt they'll ask questions. At least the cover will work in our favor."

Davis took out a set of high-powered, military-grade binoculars that did little to ease Aaron's worries. Why would a trapper have such a tool?

"They're at the edge of the woods. They'll be here soon." Davis glanced over at them. "You mind telling me what's going on here? I'm an army ranger and I've seen my share of combat situations in both Afghanistan and Iraq. This isn't just some random attack. These guys are after something and I'd like to know what I've got myself involved in."

Aaron saw Liz's warning glance and said, "Let's just say those men out there shooting at us are some very bad guys. They've killed lots of innocent people. So you can either help us, or stay out of our way. The choice is yours."

Davis stared from one to the other, he knew there was more to the story than he'd been told.

He just blew out a frustrated sigh. "Okay, what do you want to do?"

In Aaron's mind, there was only one option. "When you get a clear shot, fire," he said. Davis nodded and turned away.

Three snowmobiles stopped abruptly at the edge of the woods as if waiting for something.

"What do you think they're doing?" Liz asked uneasily.

"I'm not sure. Are they waiting for orders?" Aaron focused on the vehicles. He could see each of them held two armed men. They were outnumbered two to one, but they still had a chance as long as the men hadn't called for reinforcements.

"They're heavily armed." While he watched, the men disembarked and began spreading out through the woods. "They're fanning out," he said and turned to her. "They're going to surround us."

Liz started for the opposite window to stand guard there and in that moment it hit him like a ton of bricks. He cared about her.

Aaron clasped Liz's good hand and she turned with questions in her eyes. He could no longer deny it. In spite of all the walls he'd put up to protect his heart, Liz had gotten through.

"Keep your eyes open," he said instead of what he wanted to tell her. He shoved his feelings deep inside. Would Beth's betrayal always be there in the back of his head, preventing him from moving on? He didn't want to be held prisoner by those doubts for the rest of his life.

She presented him with a confused smile. Had she seen something in him? "I will. You too. I don't want anything to happen to you, Aaron." She turned away and he let her go along with the breath he'd held inside and prayed with all his heart for a chance to break the bondage of doubt and be the man he wanted to be...for her.

"I have an idea. Can you two cover me?" Davis asked them.

Liz and Aaron exchanged a surprised look. Even though Davis had told them he was a ranger, Liz still wasn't sure of his intentions.

"This isn't your fight. Stay low and try to keep alive," she told him. At the very least, his motives were questionable. She didn't know whose side he was really on and until she did, they couldn't afford to let their guard down for a second.

"Look, you're outnumbered. You need my help," Davis insisted. "I'm not the bad guy here," he added quietly, trying to assure them.

"What do you have in mind?" Aaron asked eventually and Liz shot him a look. He held up his hand. "We're running out of options, Liz."

She blew out a sigh and slowly nodded. Liz just hoped they weren't making a huge mistake by accepting Davis's help.

"If I can reach the woods behind the cabin,

I can circle around back behind and get a good shot without being detected. It might give us an advantage."

"Do it," Aaron said and Davis hurried out the back door.

"What are you doing? You can't rely on this guy. He's up to something," Liz said the second Davis was out of earshot.

Aaron shook his head. "I don't trust him either, but he's right. We need his help."

Liz watched as Davis kept low to the ground and crept off into the woods behind the cabin.

She followed his movement through the binoculars she'd brought in her backpack. "He's heading off to the left." She turned back to Aaron. "What do you think he wants?"

He was quick to respond. "I'm not sure. But there's no way he just showed up by accident when he did."

Liz had to agree. "Do you think he's really a ranger?" She had to admit, he carried himself like ex-military, but with so much at stake, they couldn't afford to simply take Davis at this word.

"He has an agenda," Aaron said. "The only question is what is it and how bad is it going to hurt us?"

Liz scanned the area with the binoculars. Two men were creeping along the edge of the woods to the right of the cabin. "I have two coming this way."

She saw Aaron search the area within his viewing. "Same here. That leaves two unaccounted for." The words had barely left his mouth when the men closest to him opened fire shattering the window. Aaron ducked to the right as bullets came through the cabin. Liz hit the floor. Seconds later an onslaught of shots flew through her side of the house.

Tucking low, Liz peered over the windowsill and opened fire. The men returned fire and she ducked once more. Inside the cabin it sounded like a battle zone with shots coming in all directions.

With her heart pounding, Liz waited out the onslaught. Silence followed the bombardment and she slowly eased to a sitting position. After spotting one of the men, she aimed for his leg and pulled the trigger. The man screamed in pain and hit the frozen ground hard.

"I'm hit," he yelled to his partner who rushed to his aid and dragged him into the safety of the woods.

She watched as Aaron fired off a several rounds. "I have one down," he exclaimed.

Off in the distance, multiple rounds ricocheted through the woods.

Liz and Aaron stared at each other.

"Do you think Davis is okay?" she asked, concerned.

Aaron shook his head and glanced out the shattered window. "Hang on. I see two men, I'm guessing they're the two remaining guys. It looks like they're leaving," he said in disbelief.

Liz crept over to his vantage point. The two men appeared to be running for their lives as if someone pursued them. One held his side and what appeared to be blood oozed from beneath his hand.

"He's hit," she exclaimed. She peered through the binoculars. "It looks like they're all retreating." As they watched, the men climbed on the snowmobiles and headed back in the direction they'd come.

"Thank You, God," Aaron voiced his gratitude aloud.

"Where's Davis?" she asked. Had their doubts been justified? Was Davis part of the men hunting them? Liz moved to the back door and looked out. Straight ahead and still some distance away, something glistened in the snow.

"There." Liz pointed and zeroed in through the binoculars. "There he is. He's coming this way. Aaron, I don't like it. There's something strange about him jumping on board so quickly to help us without really knowing what he's getting himself into."

"I agree. Even if he is a ranger, I don't believe his motives one little bit. Be ready," he warned.

Something had occurred to her. "He could be connected to Michael in some way. If Michael moved the weapons here, he would have had to have help."

Aaron's gaze met hers. "It makes sense. That would explain why he's so willing to help us out. Maybe he's trying to protect the guns."

Davis emerged from the woods slowly. Liz also didn't understand why he needed such a high-powered weapon for trapping.

"Hold your fire," Davis said when he drew closer and spotted their rifles. "I'm on your side, remember."

Aaron didn't take his eye off the man. "Are you. I'm not so sure. Why would a simple trapper put himself in harm's way to help two people he doesn't even know? I can't make it add up, my friend," Aaron said in a dangerous tone.

Davis's smile appeared plastered to his face. "I told you I'm military. I'm guessing you two are as well. You know you don't leave a fellow soldier behind. Like it or not, I can't forget that code of honor no matter how much it puts me at risk."

Liz didn't completely buy the story, but until they knew what he wanted, they'd need to keep him close.

Slowly she lowered her weapon and Aaron did the same.

"We appreciate the help," she said quietly.

The man slowly nodded. "After what happened, I can understand you having doubts. My heart still feels as if it's about to come out of my chest. I haven't seen this much excitement in a long time."

Davis glanced around at the destruction that had taken place in the tiny cabin and then back at them. "The previous attack was clearly not a mistake, and now within the space of just a little while, you're hit again. I'd say those men came after you for a reason."

A single muscle worked in Aaron's jaw. He was uneasy. So was she. Ranger or not, neither of them trusted Davis just yet.

"You're correct—they are after us for a reason. But for your own safety, it's best that you don't know anything more. Still, we're grateful that you came along when you did," Aaron said with a guarded edge to his voice.

Davis clearly wanted to ask more questions, but thought better of it. "Also a good break that I'm a ranger who knows when someone is up to no good."

Liz still couldn't shake the feeling that Davis hadn't told them the whole truth.

He must have read her misgivings because he pulled out his tags. "Seventy-Fifth Ranger Regiment, Second Battalion. While I might be rusty at trapping, I know when someone's in trouble."

She smiled, relieved. "We're very glad you do."

"With everything that's happened, I'm sad to say I don't know your name." He stuck out his hand to Liz. "Davis Kincaid."

"Liz Ramirez," she said and just for a second he seemed to recognize the name. Impossible, surely? They'd never met before. Still it was enough to put her on guard again.

Aaron must have sensed something as well because he moved closer to her.

If Davis noticed the gesture, he chose to ignore it. "You know they'll be back, don't you?" he said without looking at them. "Whatever their reasons for coming after you with such force, they'll be back and soon."

"That's why we need to get out of here," Liz turned to Aaron and said. "We can't stay. This is the first place they'll look when they come back."

"I went into town a couple of days ago. There are men here that I'd swear are former military," Davis told them, capturing both their attention. He was clearly fishing for answers. The only question that remained—was he one of those men? Was Davis Kincaid a friend or a foe?

TWELVE

Aaron still thought it was a little too convenient that Davis had showed up when he did. While he didn't believe the man was working for Safar, he wondered if he was the person who had assisted Michael with moving the weapons to Black Bear. If that were the case, then Aaron would do whatever he had to do to protect himself and Liz.

But Davis was correct about one thing. Those men would return.

"Liz, it's time to call in backup. Even if we make it to the cabin, they'll keep coming after us. We need help."

He was eyewitness to the battle raging inside her. "Okay. Do it," she finally said.

Aaron took out his cell phone and tried to get a signal. "Nothing," he shook his head and then glanced out the window. If he could get high enough maybe he could find a signal.

"I have a sat phone," Davis volunteered. "It usually works better up here. Cell service is pretty much nonexistent." He reached into his backpack and pulled out a satellite phone.

Liz shot Aaron a look. She had the same concerns as him. Why would a trapper, even a ranger, have a satellite phone on him?

Davis seemed to interpret their reaction. "I come here often. I like to hunt as well as trap. As much as I enjoy the solitude, I also like to be prepared. Things can go south quickly in the bush, especially this time of year." He pointed to the storm outside. "Now, maybe you'd be kind enough to fill me in on what's really happing here," he told them quietly.

Like it or not, Davis had helped save their lives and they really didn't have a choice. Under the very-best-case-scenario conditions, backup was still hours away.

Aaron attempted a smile. "Sorry for the evasion, but after what happened today, you're right. You should understand what you're involved in. Liz and I are CIA agents and we're here in Black Bear looking for some stolen weapons." He gave Davis the abridged version of why they were in Black Bear, leaving out the mention of Michael's evidence entirely.

Davis shook his head in disbelief. "I can understand why you didn't trust me."

Aaron smiled. "Yes, but we are obliged for the assistance and the use of the phone."

It took Davis a second to respond. He appeared

to be digesting what Aaron had told him. "No problem. I have some food as well. You two look as if you're traveling pretty light."

"Thanks, but we have provisions. Excuse me," Aaron said and stepped outside to make the call. While he waited for it to go through, he could hear Liz talking with Davis. She had an unassuming way of asking questions so that the person didn't realize he was being interrogated. But Davis was different. As a ranger, he'd know the tricks of the trade.

Aaron couldn't let go of the feeling that Davis was hiding something. He didn't believe he'd happened upon them by accident.

When Jase answered, he clearly didn't recognize the number. "Who is this?" he said in a hard tone.

"Brother, it's me." Aaron couldn't imagine what Jase was thinking. As the base commander, technically Jase outranked him and Liz and he had disobeyed a direct command to bring Liz in.

"Where are you?" Jase asked and Aaron could almost hear his anger warring with relief.

"We're in Black Bear, Alaska. Liz is with me." He quickly told Jase everything that had happened.

"Hang on, I'm checking the weather right now," Jase said in a grave tone. "As I'm sure you know, everything west of the Rockies has been grounded for a while. It looks as if it will lift here soon.

When it does we'll be on our way. Still, there's no guarantee we can reach Black Bear even if we do get airborne." Jase hesitated and then asked. "Do you trust this guy Davis?"

Aaron glanced back through the busted window to where Liz and Davis stood. "Not really, but he helped us out, so that's something."

"I'll see what I can find out about him and this Safar person. Looks like the closest trooper station is more than a hundred miles away. With the storm right over you at the moment, they probably won't reach you any sooner than we might. You two are on your own until we can get to you."

It wasn't the news he wanted to hear, but at least now someone knew where they were. "Anything on Rick's family?"

"They're safe. SWAT rescued them late yesterday evening. From what I understand, it was touch and go for a while. Several of the kidnappers were shot and killed. We have some in custody. Let's hope they'll shed some light on what's going on. The troopers reached Rick's cabin," Jase added. "He's safe and the bad guys are in custody."

Aaron whispered a heartfelt prayer under his breath. With all the bad happening around them, at least something good had taken place.

"Hang tight, Aaron. We'll be there as soon as we can. In the meantime, I'll do some checking on Safar and let's hope it's not an alias. I'll also run Kincaid's name by one of my ranger friends and see what I can come up with. But it seems to me if he's not against you, he must be for you." Jase paused before adding, "And when this is over, we'll discuss your actions."

Aaron smile faded. He had a feeling he wasn't going to like that conversation one little bit. "I'm praying for you two. Make sure you keep the phone close. I'm calling in the troopers as backup. I have a feeling we'll need them."

Aaron ended the call with a small sense of peace. Help was on the way; they just had to stay alive until Jase and the team arrived.

He went back inside and Liz and Davis both turned at his entrance. He could read all the questions in Liz's eyes and he smiled.

"He's on the way to Black Bear. The weather's questionable, but he thinks they'll be airborne soon. In the meantime, he has called the troopers out for backup."

She returned his smile. "We just have to hang on a little while longer."

Aaron squeezed her hand. "And I have good news. Rick's family is safe. SWAT rescued them last evening."

Suddenly laughter burst through her and tears filled her eyes. "That is good news. God is in control."

Aaron swallowed hard. Just looking at her now, exhausted beyond belief and completely unaware of how beautiful she was, it was as if God was telling him to let his mistrust go. He had a chance at happiness with Liz.

Her laughter disappeared and a confused look knitted her brows. "Aaron?" Her voice sounded… unsteady.

He shook his head. He needed time.

"I think the weather's definitely easing here a little," Davis said when an awkward silence came between them. "That will be good for your rescue team, but bad for us. It gets dark quickly at this time of year. It'll be pitch-black in a few hours. If those men don't come back before then, at the very least, we'll have to hike out of here to reach the cabin under subfreezing temperatures at night. It's going to be a near-impossible feat."

Aaron realized he was right. "All the more reason why we should get out of here while there's still daylight." He pulled out the map Paul provided. "This is where the private cabin is located," he said and pointed to the location on the map. "It butts up to the mountain, so it will make it harder for the rescue choppers to land, but we should be able to see anyone coming for some distance. It will give us an advantage. Once we make it there safely, I'll call Jase again and let him know the new location."

It was Michael's cabin, but he was deliberately keeping that information between them.

Aaron watched Davis's reaction. He could almost swear the man recognized the cabin. "Do you know the place?" Aaron asked incredulously.

Davis shook his head. "No, I'm just thinking that it will take us a couple of hours to reach it." He pointed to Liz's brace. "Are you up to it?"

That she was in pain was easy to see, but Liz wasn't one to recoil because she was injured. "I can keep up—don't worry about me."

"I have an idea that might buy us some time," Davis said. "They'll still be looking for us here." He opened his backpack and pulled out some explosives and a timer.

Aaron's blood ran cold. Michael's Jeep and cabin had been wired with explosives. In a blink of an eye, his misgivings about the man went ballistic.

Beside him, he could feel Liz tense.

"What are you doing with explosives up here?" she asked and he could tell her mind went to the same place as his.

"I prepare for everything when I come here. There are areas where avalanches happen on a regular basis. It's always good to have explosives to do a controlled blast before you get caught in one."

While his answer made sense, Aaron couldn't get the similarities between the two bombs out of his head.

Davis put the explosives on the table. "I'll set some outside along the tree line and a couple in here to detonate when the front door is breached. I hate destroying the cabin because other people sometimes use it, but I don't think we have a choice. Our backs are against the wall. We need something to give us an advantage. You two should go ahead. I'll catch up with you."

With more distrust than confidence, Aaron donned Liz's backpack and then they headed out into the cold. The snow had eased to a light peppering, but the fog had intensified. It was hard to see even a few feet in front of them.

Once they were out of earshot, Liz asked, "Do you think he had something to do with what happened at Michael's place in Painted Rock?"

His gut told him Davis wasn't part of Safar's team. "I don't think so, but he definitely has an agenda. He's deliberately keeping us close. We can't let our guard down around him, Liz."

She stopped for a second to look deep into his eyes. She touched his face. "How are you holding up?" she asked gently. Even through her own pain, she was worried about him.

Aaron stepped closer. He cared about her so much. She had made him see that there was someone who he could trust with his heart and it was her. But there were so many obstacles in their way. The biggest being whether or not they'd even survive until Jase arrived.

He covered her good hand with his and then

brought it to his lips and kissed it gently. "I'm okay. How are you?"

She blushed at the tender moment happening between them, then smiled and assured him, "I'm going to be okay."

With his heart soaring with promise, they started trudging through the deep snow.

Aaron couldn't stop wondering about Davis. He'd said he came there often so it stood to reason that he'd be more aware of the conditions than he and Liz, but all his prep seemed an overkill. And there was just something about Davis that he couldn't place that bothered him.

With fear making it impossible to relax for a moment, Aaron kept close to Liz's side. She was barely hanging on and soon the exertion of walking in deep snow took its toll.

She stumbled once and he caught her around her waist. "I've got you," he assured her gently. "Here, let me carry the rifle."

She barely had the energy to nod.

Behind them, he heard a noise and whirled around. Davis charged their way.

"I hear more snowmobiles approaching. There hasn't been enough time for your guys or the troopers to get here. It has to be them. We have to hurry, we need to be farther away so that we don't get caught up in the blast."

Aaron listened for a second and heard what

Davis had. He grabbed Liz's hand and they ran as fast as they could.

Once they were safely in the woods, Liz glanced back at their tracks.

"Between the wind and the snowfall, they should be covered quickly," Aaron said with more confidence than he felt. "They'll head for the cabin first. Once there, they'll know we're gone and figure we're on foot."

"I'll wait until some of them go inside the cabin before I detonate the rest of the explosives," Davis said. "Hopefully, we can take out their snowmobiles in the process. It will buy us some time."

The machines grew closer. "Not all of them will search the cabin. What's to keep the rest of the men from seeing what happened to their cohorts and running?" Aaron said.

Davis stared in the direction they'd come. "Unless you have a better plan, let's see what happens. With your partner's injuries we need an advantage."

"Aaron, he's right," Liz said. "We have to take the chance. It will hopefully allow us to reach the cabin undetected. And with the chaos, it should take them longer to locate which direction we went."

He hesitated a second longer before agreeing. "Okay, but you had better take all those snowmobiles out. Because if you don't, they'll know we escaped and there's no way we can hold them off until our backup arrives."

Davis pointed to a ridgeline off to the left. "I'm going to hike up there for a better vantage point. If something goes south, I'll fire off a shot." He hurried off before Aaron could stop him.

Once Davis was out of hearing range, Liz asked, "Do you believe him?" He could tell she didn't.

"Not really. I just hope he actually did wire the place and isn't leading them straight to us. I still don't trust him, Liz. If he's in cahoots with these guys, he now knows where we're heading." Aaron blew out a sigh. "Either way, we need to get going."

They started hiking at a fast pace.

"You know, there's something familiar about Davis that I can't pinpoint," Liz told him.

Aaron's gaze shot to her "You recognize him?" He hadn't really thought about it until Liz mentioned it, but Davis did seem recognizable.

She shook her head. "I'm not sure. Maybe he has that type of face and people are always mistaking him for someone else."

"Maybe," he said doubtfully. "Anyway, I'd say the sooner we get to the cabin the better. It's bad enough that we have men chasing us on snowmobiles and choppers. Now we have this guy with unknown intentions thrown into the mix."

* * *

As hard as she tried, Liz couldn't figure out what it was about Davis Kincaid, beyond his sudden appearance that made her uneasy. Something about him reminded her of someone but she couldn't place who. Yet for the time being, they were forced to trust him. She was barely hanging on, not able to pull her weight. They'd need Davis's help.

Once they reached the top of a hill, Aaron used Liz's binoculars and surveyed the area they'd left. "Their men are almost to the cabin. Looks like they're getting off their snowmobiles."

She drew in a shaky breath. "I sure hope this works."

Liz could feel her adrenaline roaring to life. She and Aaron had been on a roller-coaster ride and there were still so many questions unanswered. They swirled through her head.

"Come on, just a little bit farther away..." Aaron whispered as they watched the men fan out through the trees.

The advancing men reached the front of the cabin; one grabbed the door handle. Seconds later, the cabin went up in a firestorm. The men left standing headed for their machines. The woods where the snowmobiles were parked exploded. Pieces of the destroyed vehicles shot up in the air along with tree parts.

The men stopped dead in their tracks and stared at the devastation in shock.

"Let's get out of here," Aaron said. "We need to keep moving. We have to reach the cabin if we stand a chance at defending ourselves."

They headed through the woods as fast as they could.

"How much farther?" Liz asked, unable to hide her exhaustion.

"About another half hour," he told her and she tried to hide her disappointment.

He squeezed her shoulder. "You can do this. We've come this far. You can't give up now."

She knew she had to do whatever possible to clear her name and make sure she stayed out of jail long enough to bring Michael's killers to justice. Drawing deeply on her faith that God would show them through this passage safely, she took Aaron's hand and held it tight.

"I won't. We're in this together and that's the way we'll finish it."

The smile he gave her warmed her through and through. She'd do everything in her power to pull her weight for as long as she could.

Liz glanced behind them as the blazing inferno shot into the bitter cold air.

"There's the cabin," Aaron said with obvious relief and pointed at something ahead of them.

Liz stopped dead. She barely saw the tiny weathered cabin through the dense fog. This was it. Everything they'd done to get here was about to be worth it...if the evidence Michael left her was still there.

"Are you ready?" Aaron asked and waited for her answer. He'd seen her struggling. He had to be exhausted as well.

"I am. Let's finish this." She watched him smile at her courageous words.

"Let's. To be safe, we should circle around to the left and avoid that open area. If we head that way, it should take us to the back of the cabin."

It made sense. Right now, they were partially obscured from anyone inside. In the open, it would be a different story.

She followed him as he angled deeper into the woods. The weather had continued to worsen as they walked and Liz tried to stifle her fears. Would Jase be able to reach them in time?

Liz asked Aaron one of the questions chasing through her head. "Why would anyone choose to trap in these conditions?"

"Believe it or not, it's the best time. Animals are on the move looking for food."

She remembered Michael talking about something similar when he'd mentioned the various times he'd trapped in the past.

"It should be just over that next ridge to our right," Aaron pointed in that direction. "We're almost there."

She still clutched his hand. "Good." She wasn't

sure how much farther she could go. As they trekked up the ridge, gusts of wind barraged them with icy pellets.

The weather was closing in on blizzard conditions. The path ahead was obscured by driving snow. Her eyes watered so much that it all but blinded her. They'd been exposed to the elements for a long time. They had to be getting dangerously close to hypothermic.

"Do you see anything?" she asked Aaron when she stopped to catch her breath.

"Not yet, but we're almost right on top of the ridge." He leaned forward and strained to see ahead.

Liz didn't want to think about what might happen if they couldn't find the cabin. They'd be dead in a couple of hours. As it was, they needed to get out of the weather as quickly as possible.

Everything around them had gotten blanketed in white including the air. Several times, Aaron had been on top of an area that had sloughed away. The rocks crumbling. One false move, and they'd plunge to their deaths.

Liz tried to squash the panic rising inside her. After they'd gone a little farther, the path dipped downward into a valley and then rose.

They kept battling the roaring wind heading in the direction they'd seen the cabin. Liz squinted through the driving snow. She saw something.

"Over there." She pointed in the direction and Aaron squinted to see.

"That's it." She'd never heard him sound so relieved. "Thank You, God."

She smiled and offered her own prayer of gratefulness. Before they headed for the wooded area behind the cabin, Davis caught up with them.

He pointed to a high area that would offer a three-hundred-and-sixty-degree view of the surrounding area under normal conditions. "I'm going to have a look. Make sure no one else is coming. I have some gear stowed not far from here. Some extra weapons and food and another sat phone. We may need them. I'll be back in a couple of hours."

Liz didn't believe his excuse for a moment. In this storm, it would be nearly impossible to see anything. Aaron was right. Davis was hiding something from them. She prayed whatever it was wouldn't end up costing them their lives.

THIRTEEN

Aaron waited until Davis had disappeared from sight before saying, "He's definitely up to something. There's no way he can see anything in this storm."

She nodded in agreement. "But is he working for the men hunting us, or acting alone?"

"Whichever it is, I don't like it." He glanced down at the cabin below them. "We don't know if they've been here already..." He stopped and looked her in the eyes. "Or if there's anyone inside. We have to be careful."

Aaron focused the binoculars on the area surrounding the cabin.

"I don't see any sign that someone's been there."

Next to him, Liz did the same. "Yes, but still, the sooner we find the information Michael left and get out of here, the better."

He couldn't agree more. "How's your wrist holding up? That was a tough go back there."

She managed a smile for his sake. "It hurts, but

the brace makes it tolerable. I'll be okay, Aaron. Don't worry about me."

She was putting on a brave front, but still he knew she couldn't take much more physically or emotionally.

Aaron pointed to the back side of the cabin where it joined the woods. "We should be able to go in undetected if someone is watching the place...unless they're inside." It was a harrowing thought. They had to get in and out of the cabin as quickly as possible.

Up at the higher altitude, the snow was piled up high. Just walking a short distance was a workout. Especially for someone injured and already running on empty. They were forced to take periodic breaks that slowed their time tremendously.

When they finally reached the edge of the woods, Liz was barely hanging on.

"Wait here. Let me check the place. You're exhausted." He was seriously worried about her health. If something jumped up while they were at the cabin, he doubted her ability to defend herself.

That she rejected the suggestion was no surprise. "No, I'll be okay. I can handle myself." While he didn't believe it, he understood her stubbornness. Her future depended on finding the evidence left by Michael. She was banking her life on it.

"Take a moment to rest and catch your breath.

I'm going to do some recon." She barely managed a nod.

Aaron moved a little closer to the edge of the woods, his heart drumming a crazy beat.

"Lord, please…we need Your help. Give her the strength she needs to make it through this. Give us the answers we need. Keep us alive," he whispered the prayer and then zeroed in on the cabin with the binoculars.

The cabin's blinds were all drawn. Aaron couldn't see anything beyond the front and sides of the place. There were a couple of chairs set up on the front porch. Something about them drew his attention. It was almost as if someone had deliberately turned the chairs over. Had it been Michael? Was it some type of signal? He had a sinking feeling, but he couldn't share it with Liz. He needed her to remain positive.

He headed back to her once more.

"How does it look?" She asked the question he was expecting while watching him closely.

"It doesn't appear that anyone's been there recently. I don't see any tracks out front or leading to the woods behind the place. But then again, the snow would have covered them as well. The blinds are drawn so I couldn't see inside." He looked at her. "Be prepared."

He knew she understood. They could be facing an ambush.

Aaron took the lead as he made his way back to the lookout spot and turned to survey her appearance.

"Are you ready for this?" he asked and prayed that she was up to the task at hand.

"Yes, I'm ready." She touched his arm when he appeared uncertain. "Aaron, I've got this."

He brushed hair from her face. She was so beautiful and...he loved her. The way he reacted to her nearness. The fierce desire in him to protect her only confirmed the truth that had been there for a while. He loved her. He wanted a chance for them. For a future. But first they had to survive this and he was so afraid of losing her.

"Aaron?" She said his name tentatively and he realized she was watching him. Seeing him go through the emotions of realizing he loved her.

"I'm okay," he assured her and then slowly stepped out into the open and immediately felt a sense of exposure. Drawing in a deep breath, he slowly advanced to the back of the cabin all the while praying for their safety.

Once he reached the structure, he stepped up on the back deck. Liz handed him the key and as quietly as possible he unlocked the door.

He turned back to her and mouthed, "On my count."

She drew her weapon and waited until he'd counted off and then slowly he eased the door open. Darkness greeted them. There was no electricity. He took out his flashlight and looked around. There were a several lanterns on the kitchen table along with matches. He just hoped they'd light because he'd need to conserve the flashlight's battery. It took three tries before he was able to get one of the lanterns to burn. He quickly lit the others. And then they got their first good look inside.

Right away, Aaron's heart sank. The place looked as if it had been ransacked. Someone had turned over furniture and tossed contents haphazardly around, searching for something.

Liz covered her mouth with her hand. "We're too late," she said in a broken tone. "Aaron, we're too late."

He hurried to her side. "We don't know that. I seriously doubt that Michael left the box someplace easy to find. Let's make sure the place is clear and then we'll take a closer look around."

Liz slowly nodded, but as much as she wanted to believe him, she didn't. She took out the note Michael had left her and reread it. There was no indication as to where he'd hidden the box and she couldn't have felt more frustrated.

With lanterns in hand, they cleared the cabin of perps before taking a more detailed look at its contents. The cabin consisted of a bedroom, a bath, kitchen and tiny living space. Not much area to hide something as important as a box full of evidence.

Aaron walked around the cabin as if looking for some hidden compartment where the files might be.

"Some of these old cabins have attics. Maybe we'll find something there."

"I'll search in the bedroom." She hurried to the room and left Aaron to look around the living area.

From the light of the lantern, she saw a small bed had been shoved in the corner of the room. A lumpy mattress and a threadbare bedspread the only things on the bed frame. Liz glanced around. There was nothing else in the room. No nightstand, no closet. Frustrated, Liz held the lantern up high and glanced up at the ceiling. Something was off. Was that board slightly out of place?

"In here, Aaron," she called out and he followed the sound of her voice.

She pointed to the ceiling. "Maybe this is where he hid it?"

"Amazing," he said and then he went over and moved the bed under the loose board in the ceiling. Aaron had to stand on the edge of the bed frame so that he could reach the board. "It's definitely loose. Actually several of them are." He shoved them aside to reveal an opening.

"There's no way we can climb up there," Liz said. We need something that will get us up higher."

Aaron hopped down. "Hang on, there's a chair

in the living room that might work." He left and came back with a wooden chair and shoved the bed out of the way. "Let me go first and then I'll lift you up." It was a struggle for him to gain access to the opening.

He leaned out and held his hand to her. "Take my hand. I'll haul you up."

She grabbed hold of his with her good one and he clasped his other hand around her arm and he pulled with all his strength. Liz shot through the opening, landed on top of him, and they both tumbled backward.

"That was some landing," he told her with a strained chuckle that echoed through the attic.

Aaron got to his feet and she did the same. Liz brushed off her clothes. Dust covered everything in sight. It was pitch-black inside.

Aaron took his flashlight out of his pocket and shone it around. The room was empty. "There's nothing here," she said with disappointment in every syllable.

"Hold on. Maybe there's more to the place than what we can see."

She looked around while trying to keep a positive attitude.

The room appeared to run the length of the cabin. It was a good ten degrees warmer than the rooms below.

Liz desperately searched the walls for any

makeshift opening where Michael might have hidden the box.

Aaron went to the opposite side of the room.

"Over here," he said and she went over to where he stood. There in the dust was an impression of where something had been stored. It certainly could have been a box of some type. But whatever had been there was gone now.

"Let's get out of here," Liz said despondently. She couldn't believe they'd come all this way for nothing. She felt as if her last chance at freedom had just slipped away. They'd been counting on the evidence being the one thing that could save her and now it was gone.

Aaron came over to her. "Hey, we'll figure this out. We're not anywhere close to being done yet."

It was a struggle to pull it together, but he was being strong for her. She owed him the same.

She managed a smile and slowly nodded.

"Come on, let's go back down and see if we can piece together the facts that we know so far," she said.

Using his arms to support himself, Aaron eased through the hole and then leaped to the floor.

"You'll have to jump. I'll catch you," he told her. She couldn't put weight on her injured wrist so there was no other option. She jumped for Aaron and he caught her in his arms and eased her down to the floor.

Aaron glanced around at the dust covering

the place. "Look at the footsteps." He pointed to something they'd both missed earlier in their hurry to locate the evidence.

Their gazes tangled. "There's only a single set of footprints other than ours."

Aaron stared at the imprints. "Someone's been here recently. If it was the men chasing us there'd be more imprints. The only other person in the area that we know of is Davis…"

Liz couldn't make sense of it. "Why would he take the evidence?"

Aaron shook his head. "Maybe he stumbled on the cabin and searched it. Found the box and thought the contents might be worth something."

"I guess it's possible." But she was doubtful. Liz glanced around the place and noticed something else they'd missed in their initial search.

There were photos hanging on the walls. She took the lantern over to one of them. It was a photo of a childhood Michael…with Sam.

"Aaron…" She turned to him in shock, not believing what was right before her. Was it possible that Michael had known Sam since he was a child?

He stared up at the photo. "Unbelievable."

She met his gaze. The implication clear. "You were right. They did have a connection."

There was another photo of Michael next to it, obviously taken during his time as a marine, his arm draped around another man in uniform.

She went over to the photo. "Who's that next to Michael?"

"I don't know." Aaron appeared still in shock. "I still can't believe Michael had known Sam since they were kids."

Something occurred to her. "Aaron, there's enough proof to tie Michael to Sam right here on these walls. Maybe we don't need the rest of the evidence."

FOURTEEN

Aaron glanced past Liz to the photos that were displayed. "The only problem is, all the photos prove is that Michael knew Sam. It doesn't exonerate you. You could still have been part of the plan."

Her face fell. "That's right. I don't know what to do." Her hand swept the photos. "This can't be all there is. Michael was very clear in his note and it appears there was something hidden in the attic."

Aaron recalled Michael's irrational behavior. Maybe there was nothing in the box. Had Michael lied to Liz to get her up here for a reason? If so, then for what end? So many questions raced through his head.

They were missing something. "When did Michael write the note?" Aaron asked.

She thought about it for a second. "I don't know. I'm guessing while he was in the hospital. You can tell from his handwriting that he wrote it in a hurry."

"If Michael were involved in the weapons disappearing, and I think we can agree it's likely, then was it by Sam's orders or was Michael acting on his own?" He recalled what Liz had said about the time Sam held them hostage. Michael had been taken away for almost the entire day.

Aaron could see that she hated thinking of Michael's betrayal. "The only way Michael would do such a thing is if he had no other option. Aaron, I think he may have been blackmailed."

He'd thought the same thing. "That would explain why Sam was so furious with Michael. He was trying to do the right thing. He just died before he could square things."

Aaron blew out a sigh. "But where did he hide the shipment? Obviously they're not here and I don't see how one person could move them."

Liz stared out into the darkness as a heavy fog completely engulfed the cabin. "Looks like we're stuck here for a while."

"I'm going to try to reach Jase again. Let him know our new location. Maybe he has some good news." Aaron realized he still had the sat phone that Davis had given him. In all the chaos, he must have forgotten to ask for it back. He took it out but couldn't get a signal. "The weather must be messing with the satellite signal. Maybe if we can get up a little higher, the phone will pick up service."

"It's worth a try." She glanced at her watch.

"Where's Davis anyway? Shouldn't he be getting back soon?"

He studied her worried face. "Why don't you stay here? I'll go and see if I can reach Jase and then confirm our coordinates." Before she could answer, a photo on the kitchen wall caught his attention and he took one of the lanterns over for a closer look. "Is this who I think it is?"

Liz stood next to him. "That's Davis. He knew Michael from the past just like Sam. Do you think he helped Michael hide the weapons?"

There was one more photo hanging nearby, one that turned out to be the most frightening of all. Aaron couldn't believe his eyes. Was he seeing things? "That's... Alhasan."

Liz followed his line of sight. "Sam's second-in-command with Michael. Who's the man next to him?"

Aaron took the photo off the wall. "I don't know. They look an awful lot alike, though."

He felt as if they had more questions than answers.

"I have an idea," she told him and he gathered his straying thoughts.

"What is it?"

"If we can get up high enough to get cell service, we can take pictures of the people in these photos. Jessie knew Michael and she's lived here for a while. Maybe she can help us identify them and tell us how Michael knew them."

With the weather getting worse by the minute, he wasn't holding out much hope on the phone working, but they had to try. He took Liz's cell phone, snapped the photos in question and headed for the door when she stopped him.

"I'm coming with you."

The sincerity written on her face melted his heart. It reminded him again that she was nothing like Beth. Liz's character ran deep and he was so afraid he'd lose her.

"I don't think that's a good idea. You're hurt and exhausted. Climbing that ridge is going to be a challenge in this weather."

She squared her shoulders and didn't back down. "I'm still coming with you."

He stepped closer. Their eyes held. He could read all of her doubts. She didn't understand this change in him. He drew her closer. He'd give anything for this to be over. But would he find a happy ending with her?

Aaron drew in an unsteady breath, he cupped her chin and kissed her with all the love growing in his heart.

He just caught her shaky sob before she kissed him back and his heart soared. He wanted to shut out the danger that was stalking them and stay in this exact moment forever. But it was not to be for now. He ended the embrace, but still didn't move. They stared at each other, their breathing mirrored. All of her vulnerabilities were there for him to see.

He let her go. "Here, take my extra flashlight in case we get separated. Try to stay close to me and keep your eyes open. It's dark out and the storm will deafen any sound. If someone comes after us, we may not hear them until they're right on top of us."

"I will," she promised and touched her fingers against his lips and smiled.

With his heart full of emotion, Aaron opened the door and they struggled against the biting wind.

He could barely see more than a foot in front of him, but he headed in the direction of the ridge they'd come down, all the while praying the call would go through and they would find some answers.

Talking was impossible. The wind howled around the trees and slammed into them like a lethal weapon.

To keep the uncertainties at bay, Aaron occupied his thoughts with the missing box. If Davis had taken it what had he hoped to gain by it?

With nothing but a dead end, he focused on the photos and tried to wrap his head around the fact that Michael had known both Sam and Alhasan.

Aaron was exhausted and thinking clearly was nearly impossible. He focused on putting one foot in front of the other until he reached the top of the ridge.

"Please, Lord, we need help here. Let the call go through," he said aloud.

Liz stood next to him and he wrapped her in his arms for added warmth.

It took three tries before he found a signal. He dialed Jessie's number. There was so much static on the line that he barely heard the ring.

"Hello?" Jessie answered through a whirlwind of static.

"Jessie, its Aaron. I don't have much service so I'll be brief. I'm going to try to send you some pictures. I need you to tell me if you know any of the people in them."

She said something indistinguishable.

"I'm going to hang up now and text the pictures to you. Call me back when you have them." He disconnected the call without hearing her answer and quickly loaded the pictures in a text. It took forever for the pictures to load and just as long for the message to go through.

While they waited, Aaron tried to call Jase, but the connection was so bad that he wasn't sure the call had even connected.

"Jase, can you hear me?" he shouted into the phone over the roaring wind. Jase's response broke up. He heard only a couple of indistinguishable words before the call was lost.

"I can't make out anything." Aaron tried the

number again and it sounded like it connected but he couldn't hear a response. He shook his head. "I think they may be airborne. There's a lot of background noise on his end and this storm isn't helping. I'm going to try texting the coordinates for the cabin to him. Perhaps the text will go through easier than a call."

He quickly typed in the information and waited for a response.

Aaron never was so happy to read, On our way.

He showed the text to Liz. "They're on their way."

He glanced around at the burgeoning all-out whiteout facing them. Given the darkness, he was worried they might not be able to make it back to the cabin.

His thoughts fractured. Garbling pieces of information. Confusing facts. Hypothermia was close. His feet were growing numb. He had to get them out of this weather soon. Where was Jessie? Why hadn't she called back? What if she couldn't get through?

"Jessie should have received the photos by now. What's taking so long?" Liz voiced his concerns aloud while casting an anxious glance around the area. If someone were watching them, they'd seen where they were. If they were trying to kill them, they'd be sitting ducks.

Aaron pulled the photos up one at a time. The background of the one with Sam and Michael drew his attention to it. They stood close to a cabin. Was it his imagination or was it the same they'd just been in? There was only a portion of the structure showing and it was taken at a different time of the year, but the mountain in the background sure looked like Black Bear Mountain.

His phone rang and he answered the call quickly and held it so that it was sheltered against the wind and Liz could still hear.

"It's me," Jessie said. "I have the photos." Something was terribly wrong. There was no mistaking the fear in Jessie's tone.

Liz's gazed locked with Aaron.

"What is it?" Aaron asked urgently. "Do you recognize any of the photos?"

Liz knew he hated rushing the woman, but they didn't have a lot of service and it could end at any moment.

"The first one is of Michael and Sam Hendricks. Sam lived in Black Bear for a while."

Hendricks? They knew Sam as Lansford. Liz couldn't believe it. He'd changed his name at some point, which would explain why they hadn't been able to find out much about his past.

How had he managed to fake the CIA's background check? He'd had to have created an elaborate fake identity for himself. Which seemed to indicate he'd planned such an endeavor for a long time.

Incredible. At least they had a name to go by, which might lead to locating of the weapons.

"Sam left here a few years before Michael moved back to Montana."

"When was this?" Aaron asked.

"Shortly after we graduated from high school. Sam was a year older than Michael and myself."

"What about the second photo of Michael with the two men?" Liz rushed on. As much as she needed more information on Sam, she wanted to know how Michael knew Alhasan.

"You mean the one of Michael with the Safar brothers?" Jessie asked innocently enough.

The Safar brothers. The man in the photo with Michael was Alhasan's brother.

It was hard to control her excitement. They were finally getting some answers. "Yes. Who are they and how did Michael know them?"

"Their names are Alhasan and Kalel Safar. I never met them myself, but Michael told me about them once. He said they lived in Anchorage but fished the area. Michael earned extra money whenever he could by acting as a fishing guide. He was really quite good at it."

Liz recalled Alhasan had given a fake last name as well. They were uncovering more webs of lies. This whole case stunk of them.

So Michael knew Alhasan and his brother. Kalel Safar had to be the one in charge of the men chasing them and the intended owner of the weapons.

"What about Sam? Do you know if he knew the brothers?" Aaron asked. It was too big of a coincidence otherwise. The pieces were finally falling into place.

"Yes. Sam went fishing with them several times. He said the four of them were friends. My understanding was they hung out together sometimes."

Liz's first instinct was to ask more questions about Sam, but they needed to know about the remaining two photos. "What about the other photos?" she asked.

"I don't know who the marine is, but the other photo may be of Michael's brother."

Aaron's gaze locked on hers. Davis was Michael's brother.

The phone lost service and Jessie was gone.

"No," Liz said in annoyance. A few seconds later the phone rang.

"Sorry. As I said, I never met Michael's brother before. He'd left home by the time I moved to Black Bear. Michael told me once that they weren't very close." There was so much static on the call it was impossible to hear for a moment.

"After we graduated from high school, Michael's father passed away," Jessie was saying. "He took his body back to Montana for burial and I never saw him again until a few years back when he came here to fish. He and his family once rented the cabin back when they first came to Black Bear. Six months ago when Michael came back, he paid cash for it."

In spite of all the information Jessie had provided, they still didn't know who was responsible for Michael's and Sam's deaths and Liz was no closer to clearing her name than when they'd first arrived.

Jessie paused for a second. "Does Michael's death have anything to do with something Sam might have gotten him involved in?"

The question struck Liz as odd.

"Why would you say that?" she asked.

"Because Sam was always causing problems in high school. He got expelled several times, and then during the summer of his senior year, he just left the area completely and I never saw him again. I asked Michael about him, but he said he didn't want to talk about it."

"Can you think of anything else that might help us find Michael's killer?" Aaron asked but the phone cracked and then went dead.

Aaron checked the service. "It's gone." He tried the sat phone, but it wasn't any better.

"We can't stay out here in this cold any longer. We need to get back to the cabin while we can," Liz said.

Slowly they headed down the ridge, but the driving wind and snow made it impossible to see more than a few feet in front of them even with using the flashlights.

"I can't even see the cabin," Liz said over the noise of the storm. "Are we heading the right way?"

Aaron stopped to catch his breath. "I think so, but it's hard to tell. It should be just a little ways up ahead."

She wasn't sure how much farther she could go. Just drawing air burned her chest. If they lost their way in the storm, they'd be dead soon.

"Over there." Aaron pointed his flashlight at the dark mass amongst ahead of them.

As they drew closer, Liz saw something alarming. Fresh tracks that had been made since they left the cabin.

Aaron drew his weapon and she did the same. She understood. They could be walking into an ambush.

He motioned for her to go to the back of the cabin and she nodded and headed that way.

Liz edged along the side of the cabin until she could see into the window at the back. From the light of the lanterns they'd left burning, there was no movement within. She slowly eased to the door, opened it, and slipped inside. Seconds later, Aaron did the same with the front entrance. They stared at each other across the room. She shook her head.

He motioned to the single bedroom and she understood. He'd search there. She followed close behind and tapped his shoulder and pointed to the bathroom ahead.

Aaron slowly opened the bedroom door and she slipped past him into the bathroom. The tiny room was empty.

She hurried back to the bedroom as Aaron emerged. "There's no one here," he said in a chilly tone she couldn't associate with Aaron.

She ignored her misgivings for the moment. "We need to get warm. My feet are soaked."

Aaron went over to a cast-iron woodstove in the corner of the living room. Someone had piled some wood next to it. "This won't last for long," he said as he stacked wood into the stove without looking at her.

"There's more around back," she said. "Someone prepared for the winter."

Aaron flinched at the comment. She didn't understand this sudden change in him.

"You think Michael planned to come up before the accident happened?" he asked.

"Maybe. The only question is why did he want to put the cabin in my name?"

Aaron still didn't look at her. "I don't know."

The fire finally caught and he pulled up a couple of chairs close to it. "Take off your boots and socks and let's warm our feet. We don't want to lose a toe due to frostbite."

As the storm continued to batter the cabin, Liz thought about everything that Jessie had told them.

"Why do you think Michael pretended not to know Sam?"

Aaron shook his head, staring into the fire. "There's only one reason I can think of."

She knew exactly what he was talking about. She just hated thinking her friend and partner had been working for the Fox all this time.

"I still can't believe he knew Alhasan. Where's the brother? He has to be the one chasing the weapons."

"Probably. Where's Michael's note?" he asked unexpectedly in a sharp tone.

She didn't understand why he needed to see it, but she pulled it out and gave it to him.

"Now that I've thought about it some more there's something odd about this note," he told her and she didn't understand what he meant.

She watched him read through the note once more.

"Like what?" she asked while trying to understand the change in him.

The chill in his eyes when he looked at her scared her. "The handwriting. I've seen lots of memos and comments written by Michael. This doesn't look like his handwriting, Liz. I'm not so sure he was the one who wrote it."

FIFTEEN

He believed her...in his heart, but his common sense was screaming there were too many things off in her story.

"What are you saying?" The hurt in her eyes was hard to take. She'd seen the misgivings he couldn't cover.

"I mean I'm not so sure Michael wrote the note you have. You knew Michael better than any of us? Didn't you notice the difference in the handwriting?"

"Aaron, you're scaring me," she said in a strained voice. "I've told you everything I know. I'm not involved in Michael's death and I certainly didn't have anything to do with the missing weapons."

He wanted to believe her. He handed her the piece of paper. "I found this near the bed," he said quietly. "I guess it was tucked under the mattress and fell out when I moved the bed that last time. When I went back just now, it had fallen on the floor. The lantern's light caught it."

She took it from him. Her hands shook as she read aloud the letter that was clearly written by Michael.

"'I'm so sorry I got you involved in this, Liz. I wish I could change things. Turn back time to before this all started, but I can't. Just know that you are like family to me and I never wanted you to become part of this.'"

She looked back at him and he could see the tears in her eyes. The note indicated that Michael had been involved in Sam's crimes for quite some time. The cabin itself was probably paid for with blood money.

Frustrated, Liz said, "I understand how this looks, but I'm telling you I'm not involved in any of this, Aaron. Everything about what has happened is just as much of a surprise to me as it is to you," she managed.

Aaron swallowed. "I want to believe you, but you see how this looks. Liz, the handwriting is different from the other note Michael left you."

She shook her head. "I see that and I can't explain it. I understand what you're saying. The handwriting in the note he left me does look different. More hurried. Maybe he wrote it in a rush…I don't know." She looked him in the eyes. "Aaron, I'm just asking you to trust the person you know I am. I'm not part of this, Aaron," she pleaded. "And I can't explain the difference in the handwriting, only that I believe he must have written it in a hurry."

His heart didn't want to believe she could betray him or her country.

With his emotions raw, he leaned over and touched his head against hers. "We keep this new note out of the investigation for now. No one sees it," he said quietly.

She smiled a little, yet part of him still had doubts. Beth's destructive influence in his life had left its mark. With everything inside him, he shoved the doubts aside. He was going against every part of his training now, because he wanted to believe her.

She touched his face with her hand and he looked deep into her tear-filled eyes.

"Thank you," she whispered in a shaky breath. His heart was aching to comfort her, so despite his misgivings about her involvement, Aaron leaned forward and kissed her.

She kissed him back and he had to believe she had feelings for him as well. He'd give anything for this to all be over and they'd be free to talk about those feelings.

In the past, she'd told how devastating Eric's death had been for her. Was she finally ready to love again?

Please, God, yes.

Liz ended the kiss and stared with wonderment into his eyes. He could read all the questions, the uncertainties in hers and he smiled tenderly. He wanted to reassure her what he felt had nothing to do with the circumstances they faced.

She got to her feet and moved a little away. "I—I think Jessie packed a couple of extra pairs of socks in the backpack," she said unsteadily, then she dug in and pulled out a pair for each of them.

"Liz…" He followed her. They had no idea of the danger facing them or if they'd even make it out alive. He wanted to tell her how he felt.

He turned her to face him. "You're wrong," he said and she stared up at him. He prayed that was hope in her eyes. "What's happening between us isn't just because of the danger we're facing. I care about you, Liz." She closed her eyes briefly and when she would have pulled away he said, "No, listen to me. We may not walk out of here alive, so I want you to know…" He hesitated for a second then laid it all on the line. "How I feel. I…love you."

A sob escaped her and she covered her mouth with her trembling hand.

"I wasn't sure I'd ever feel this way again," he continued, "but I'm so glad that I do. And I know how you cared for Eric, and I know you may need time. That's okay." He smiled down at her. "I just want you to know I'm ready when you are, and I'm not going anywhere."

He drew her into his arms and held her close, just happy to embrace her for the moment.

"I care about you too, Aaron, but you're right. I need more time."

The words were not what he wanted to hear and they tore at his heart. But he'd be patient. She pulled away and looked deep into his eyes. "I'm sorry," she said in earnest.

He shook his head. "Don't be. I want you to be sure."

She nodded and moved to the window. After a moment, she said, "It looks like the storm is letting up."

He came and stood beside her. Only darkness and their own images appeared in the window.

"I'm going to text Jase again. See how far out they are." He sent the message and waited for a response that didn't come.

"Anything?" she asked and he shook his head.

Through the window's reflection, their eyes met. "Where is Davis anyway? It's been hours. It'll be daylight soon. Do you think he's left? We need that evidence. Without it we have nothing."

He'd thought the same thing. "Wherever he is, our best chance at survival is to stay put. We can't afford to go tramping around in the dark. Davis knows the area. We don't. I can't imagine where he might have hidden the evidence. And more importantly, why would he take it? It would be of no use to him…unless he planned to use the evidence to blackmail Kalel Safar."

She turned to face him. "Or worse. Aaron,

maybe he's planning to kill Safar because he took Michael's life."

He tried not to show his reaction. "Hey," he said and tugged her closer. "These are all just assumptions. Davis may not even know about the evidence or Michael's death. We'll figure out what's going on here. One way or another, Jase is on the way and he could be here soon. With everything that's happened, no one's going to believe you're involved in this, Liz. It's almost over."

She closed her eyes and leaned into him while he prayed with all his heart that he hadn't just lied to her.

Fragmented theories swam in her head. One thing didn't make sense. If Davis was the enemy, then why hadn't he removed the photo connecting him to Michael?

She shivered uneasily. The snow had started back up again. It felt as if they'd been waiting for years.

Aaron came over to where she sat close to the fire and placed his hand on her shoulder.

"Do you think Jase got the text?" she asked and tried to keep her misgivings out of her tone.

"It doesn't matter. Regardless of whether he got the text, we know they're on their way. It's only a matter of time before they reach us."

Liz tried to hold on to that hope, but she had a bad feeling that time was running out for them.

She smiled up at him. "Thank you, Aaron. I know you still have your doubts and I can't blame you. If the situation were reserved, I'd probably do the same."

He knelt next to her and she saw his love for her shining in his eyes. "We'll find the truth. I believe we're close."

She wanted to believe him. She didn't.

"Liz," he said in a broken tone before he gathered her close.

She needed to stay strong. "You're right. We'll figure it out. This is almost over." She wished more than anything that she believed her own words.

Liz barely got the words out when she heard it. The noise of multiple choppers moving in.

"That has to be Jase," Aaron said and rushed to the window. Two spotlights searched the ground close to the cabin looking for a landing spot.

Liz raced to his side and squinted through the lights trying to spot proof positive that it was their commander and not the enemy.

Before the choppers landed, the back door flew open and she and Aaron turned, startled, and watched as Davis raced inside and slammed the door closed.

"They've found us," he said, out of breath.

Shocked, Liz couldn't believe what he'd said. "No, those are our people."

Davis shook his head. "You're wrong. Get away from the window."

Liz looked at Aaron with hopelessness churning in her stomach. He quickly opened the door and gazed up at the lights. A barrage of bullets riddled the ground and he rushed inside.

"He's right. They're not ours," he said in a tight voice.

There was no time to ask where Davis had been for so long. They needed all the help they could get if they stood a chance of surviving the attack.

"I saw them when I was heading back this way. They weren't coming from town but from an area south of here."

Aaron pointed the weapon at Davis's head. "Why didn't you tell us you were Michael Harris's brother?"

"Are you crazy, man? We're about to be attacked because of something you two did and you're questioning me?"

"That's not an answer. If I'm about to die here tonight, I'd like to know who you're really working for."

"Aaron," Liz exclaimed and he glanced her way.

"I didn't tell you because I wasn't sure I could trust you," Davis murmured quietly and Aaron slowly lowered his rifle.

Liz could see it wasn't so easy for him to let go of his misgivings.

"This is not the time," he said in a dead serious tone before he stepped closer to Davis. "But I'm warning you, if you're not on the up-and-up, you'll regret the day you met me."

The two men's animosity permeated the space between them.

Davis slowly nodded. "Fair enough."

Aaron grabbed the sat phone and tried Jase's cell. She could tell from his expression that the call never made it through.

He shook his head. "We're on our own." He took her uninjured hand and looked deep into her eyes and she saw it. Aaron would be there for her, no matter how their story ended.

SIXTEEN

"Stay behind me," Aaron told Liz. "If things go bad, get out of here." He was going to do everything in his power to protect her, even if it cost him his life.

She immediately shook her head. He knew she wouldn't leave him behind.

"No, Aaron. We've come this far together. If we don't make it out, we'll die together. I'm not leaving you."

He drew in a sharp breath. The look in her eyes was heartbreaking because it held so much promise.

Aaron pulled in a breath. "Then let's take care of these guys once and for all, prove your innocence and find out why this shipment of weapons was so important."

He just got the words out when a round of bullets pierced the side of the cabin taking out windows and putting bullet-sized holes in the door and walls.

All three of them hit the floor. Aaron covered Liz's body with his. He could feel the wind from the shots close to his head and he prayed with all his heart for their safety. It felt like an eternity before silence followed.

"They're protecting themselves while they land," he whispered close to her ear. "They'll storm the place when they're on the ground. We have to be prepared." He didn't want to say it, but he believed she understood. Without intervention, their chances of surviving were slim.

She hugged Aaron tightly, not wanting to let him go. This might be the last time they were able to share their feelings and there was so much she wanted to say.

"I…love you," she whispered with tears falling from her eyes. "When you said it earlier I was shocked and scared and I'm so sorry for that. But I want you to know, I love you."

He touched her cheek. "Don't be sorry. I love you, too, Liz."

Her heart soared with happiness. If they didn't make it out, they'd die knowing they loved each other. If they survived, she'd fight with everything she had inside her to prove her innocence so that she and Aaron could have a future together.

"They're almost on the ground," Davis shouted over his shoulder.

Aaron scrambled to the nearest window and opened fire while Liz did the same.

The first chopper landed under heavy gunfire, followed shortly by the second. Both pilots quickly shone their spotlights directly at the cabin, making it impossible to see anything.

"We're at a disadvantage," Liz said and fired at first one spotlight and then the other. As a sharpshooter, she made easy work out of taking out both the lights, evening the playing field for the moment.

They continued to fire on the men exiting the two choppers, taking out several in the process.

A bullet whizzed past her head and struck Davis's arm. He yelped in pain and dropped his weapon.

Liz hurried to his side. He held his upper arm. Blood had begun to soak through his shirt and onto his jacket.

"How bad is it?" she asked.

"I'm not sure," he said before more shots were fired.

She whirled and fired, but there were too many. Half a dozen men advanced through the busted window. Just as many by way of the front door.

"Drop your weapons if you want to live," one of the men ordered.

Liz glanced at Aaron and he slowly nodded.

They were outnumbered. They'd done their best to stand off the men but it was an impossible situation.

She slowly dropped her weapon on the floor and Aaron did the same. More men stormed the cabin.

"Keep your hands were we can see them," the man ordered again and motioned to several of his underlings who took their weapons from them. They were now at their attackers' mercy.

With their weapons secured, the men stood on guard as if waiting for someone. A few minutes later, another piece of the puzzle fell into place. A tall man dressed in heavy camo stepped into the room. And there was no mistaking his identity. She'd seen him in the photo. This was Kalel Safar, Alhasan's brother.

Kalel stopped in the middle of the cabin and looked around in distaste. "I thought I'd seen the last of this place," he said smugly then stopped in front of Liz. "And you…" He shook his head. "Enough games. You will tell me where my weapons are and you will do it now." Her blood ran cold.

When she couldn't speak, Kalel motioned to one of the men standing close to her and he yanked her to her feet, clasping her arm in a vice grip.

Pain shot from her injured wrist. Kalel smiled

with pleasure. "You know that Sam was supposed to deliver them earlier and he missed our delivery date. He always was a loose cannon. Your partner was supposed to keep him in line, but he failed."

Before she'd been convinced Michael was working for Sam. Now, with the brothers' connection to Michael undeniable, she knew he'd been working for Kalel. Did Michael help Sam move the weapons and double-cross Kalel or was there something else going on?

"Now, let's try this again. Where did you hide my weapons?" Although he smiled, there was nothing humorous about the question. Kalel's fury simmered just below the surface.

"I don't know where the weapons are. Michael didn't tell me anything."

Kalel shook his head. "You disappoint me. It's your choice. If you want to help me and live, or if you want cling to your innocence and die along with your friends."

Terror filled her and she fought to free her arm from her captor, but it was useless. "I can't tell you what I don't know."

"Too bad," he said without emotion. "But one of you will talk. That person will live." He headed for the door. "Wait." Liz stopped him. She couldn't let him get away.

Kalel turned back to her, furious. "What?" he barked.

Liz shivered and nodded to Davis who held his arm. "He needs medical attention right away."

Kalel cast a disinterested look in Davis's way and then suddenly he appeared to recognize him. "Ah, the brother." He smirked. "You don't remember me since you'd already left the area by the time Alhasan and I immigrated to the US."

Davis focused on Kalel. He appeared to recognize the man at last.

"So, you remember. Your father's funeral. My brother and I were there. Along with Sam." Davis nodded. "Your brother was weak. I should have never trusted him to insure the delivery." He stepped closer.

"I enjoyed killing Michael myself." Kalel smiled with satisfaction and Liz saw the pain on Davis's face.

Davis charged for Kalel, but one of Kalel's men struck him with the butt of his weapon and immediately Davis dropped to the floor unconscious.

Kalel didn't blink an eye at the brutality. "It's light enough outside to begin the search. Michael must have hidden the weapons around here somewhere. I remember there's a cave on the side of the mountain. We'll start there." He pointed to four men. "Stay with them. If they try anything, kill them. The rest of you come with me. We have to hurry. No doubt they've called in backup."

The man holding Liz's arm released her and

gave her a shove before he left with Kalel. She stumbled and dropped to the floor close to Davis.

The four remaining men eyed them with contempt.

Aaron eased closer to where she knelt next to the unconscious Davis.

"That's close enough," one of their guards snapped. "Don't try anything foolish. You heard the boss. It will be our pleasure to kill any of you."

Davis slowly regained consciousness and tried to sit up. "Don't move," she urged. He'd lost a lot of blood. "He needs help. He'll die without it," Liz told one of the men standing guard.

The man clearly was disinterested. "He's going to be dead soon enough."

She flinched at the callousness. "At least let me slow the bleeding," she pleaded.

"Do what you like, just don't try anything."

"I'm going to ease your jacket off," she told Davis.

He managed a nod. "Okay, but be careful. It hurts all the way to my back."

She stared at him for a second and then realized he was sending her a message. She felt around. He'd tucked a Glock behind his back.

"I will. I need Aaron to help me," she told her captor. "I can't get the jacket off without his help."

The man didn't respond and she took his silence for consent. Aaron crept to the right of Davis.

"We have to be careful. The pain is bad." She

waited until the men watching them began talking amongst themselves. Her gaze cut to the Glock and Aaron saw it.

"You take this side," he indicated the one closest to the weapon.

"Sorry, this is going to hurt," she told Davis and slowly eased the jacket from his injured arm taking the Glock with her. She shoved the jacket behind Davis's head while Aaron examined the injury.

"It's not so bad," he assured Davis once he'd ripped the shirt away from the wound. "The bullet's still in there. We need to stop the flow of blood, though."

Aaron tore strips of Davis's shirt and tied it as tight as he could. "How does that feel?"

"It's okay. I think I can use it," he said and Liz understood what he was trying to convey. If they were going to fight their way out of this, Davis would be ready and able to help.

Aaron glanced at the men. They appeared to be watching something outside. He cocked his head in their direction and mouthed. "It's now or never."

One of the men turned their way as if suspecting something.

"Thanks, that feels better," Davis told Aaron. After another suspicious look, the man returned to his conversation.

"Ready?" Aaron mouthed once more. Liz swallowed and looked deep into his eyes.

She slowly nodded.

Aaron and Davis charged the two closest men. Before they had time to react, Liz fired at another. The shot struck the man through the heart. He dropped to the floor lifeless. The second man charged for the door. She fired again and he grabbed his arm, his weapon flying from his hand.

Liz snatched the man's weapon and saw Davis struggling to overpower one of the men.

"Stop right there," she ordered and aimed the weapon at his head.

Seeing that he was outmanned, he slowly lowered his weapon to the floor.

Aaron quickly gained control of the last man.

"I've rope in my backpack," Davis told them. "We need to restrain them otherwise they'll alert the others once we're gone." He grabbed the rope from his backpack. "I sure hope one of you can fly a chopper?"

Aaron tossed some of the rope to Liz and smiled. "As it happens, we both know a thing or two about them."

SEVENTEEN

Once the men were restrained Aaron and Liz gathered up their weapons and phones. Aaron peered out at the dawn. "We need to get out of here now. There's no way the rest of those men didn't hear the shots. Let's head for the chopper closest to the cabin."

Grabbing Davis around his waist, Aaron raced out of the cabin with Liz at his heels. He helped the injured man inside and engaged the engine. It took only a second to familiarize himself with the instrument panel and then they were airborne.

Aaron barely had time to clear the treetops when a handful of Kalel's men raced from the woods, firing on them.

"Hang on," he shouted over the noise. "I'm going to try an evasive move."

He jerked the chopper to the left and away from the men, but it wasn't enough. A barrage of bullets struck the chopper. They were hit.

"We're going down," he yelled as the engine

sputtered and the fuel gage dropped. A bullet had struck the fuel tank.

Aaron spotted a break in the trees and aimed for it. "Hold onto something. This is going to be a hard landing."

Even with all his training, it was an impossible feat to feather the chopper to a decent landing. They hit the ground with tremendous force and plowed ground until they hit a group of trees in front of them, forcing the chopper to a jarring halt.

"Is everyone okay?" he asked, while he searched Liz's face. He couldn't lose her like this.

"We're okay," she assured him.

They'd barely gotten airborne before taking fire. It wouldn't take the men long to find them even on foot.

"We need to get out of here as quickly as possible," he told them. "The fuel tank was hit. We're sitting on a bomb that could go off at any moment."

Aaron unbuckled his harness, opened the door, and jumped out. He helped Liz from the chopper. It took both of them to get a wounded Davis to the ground. Aaron slung his arm around Davis's waist and headed for tree coverage. "How are you holding up?" he asked. The man was as white as a sheet.

"I'm okay," Davis struggled to convince him. "I think I can keep up."

He didn't sound nearly as confident as Aaron hoped. But they were out of options.

"We have to keep moving. They'll be here soon. We still have the sat phone. If we can find a spot with decent reception we can call Jase and tell him what's happened. Have him meet us someplace else." He tried to sound positive, but the chances of them being able to escape with Davis injured were slim.

Aaron racked his brain trying to remember the details of the map. He recalled seeing one of the hunter's cabins a couple of miles away. "There's a cabin not far from here." He tried the sat phone without any luck.

A helicopter was closing in and Aaron hurried everyone deeper in the woods.

"It's looking for a place to land." It was no longer an option to leave the area. If they stood a chance at surviving, they'd have to stand and fight.

The chopper circled the wreckage, its spotlight searching the ground.

"They're trying to see if there are any survivors," Liz said in a tense voice.

The chopper circled a few more times before it landed in the open space close to the downed machine.

Half a dozen men exited, heavily armed.

"Find them," Aaron recognized Kalel's voice right away. "We still don't have the location of the weapons. Don't let them get away."

Aaron glanced around. He had to think of something quickly. A standoff was out of the question. They were grossly outmanned. He watched the men close in on the chopper. He could think of only one option.

"I have an idea. Once those men get close enough to the chopper, I'll shoot for the fuel tank. The explosion should give us a chance, but we'll need to charge the chopper and take down Kalel and whatever men there are left inside. We need to take Kalel alive to find out what he knows about the missing weapons."

Liz's gaze met his. He could see she understood it was a longshot at best, but she never let on. "That's a good idea. Do you need some help?"

Her wrist had to be hurting like crazy. Still she was the best shot around.

"Are you up to it?" he asked.

"I've got this," she assured him. And she sighted in the assault rifle. He held his breath. She was waiting until the last possible moment.

She fired once; the chopper exploded. Screams could be heard.

"Now," Aaron said and they raced for the remaining chopper.

Kalel was strapped in the seat watching the fireball in front of him and taken completely by surprise.

He whirled around but not in time.

"Drop the weapon, Kalel. You'll never get a shot off." Aaron ordered. Liz had her rifle pointed at the one remaining man on board. "Tell your man to drop his gun."

Kalel stared at them with venom before slowly issuing the order.

"Your turn, Kalel," Aaron demanded.

"My men will be here soon. You'll never get airborne."

"Nice try, but the ones that aren't hurt won't be coming to your aid," Liz said.

Aaron waited through several tense moments when he wondered if Kalel with nothing to lose wouldn't just fire on them.

Then slowly, Kalel lowered the weapon. "Fine, but you'll never make it out of Black Bear. I have men everywhere."

"Then it will be our pleasure to take them down as well." Aaron pointed to the seat belt. "Get up. We're going back to the cabin."

Under Liz's watchful eye, Kalel moved to the back seat. Along with the second man. Davis took the seat next to Aaron.

"Ready?" he asked and he could see her happiness.

She smiled genuinely. "More than ready. Let's get out of here."

He laughed for the first time in what felt like forever. It was so good to see her smile. To know that the future held a promise it hadn't before. They might not be out of the woods yet, but it was as if the weight of the world had lifted.

They had the person responsible for buying the weapons. Whatever evil plans Kalel had for them, it wouldn't happen now. They'd find out where the weapons had ended up along with the evidence Michael had left behind, because in Aaron's mind, Davis knew exactly where they were at.

"Why did you kill Michael?" Liz asked the biggest question on her mind. She needed to know why her partner had to die.

Kalel stared at her with a dead expression. "Why would I tell you anything?"

"To help yourself. If you talk, it could mean you won't get a death sentence."

Kalel wasn't moved by her answer. "You're so sure you've won. This isn't over, Agent Ramirez."

Aaron jerked briefly around to stare at Kalel. "What are you talking about?"

Kalel merely smirked.

Aaron had reached the cabin. He zeroed the spotlight in on the surrounding area. "I don't see anything, do you?"

Liz focused on the woods around the cabin. "Hang on." She spotted movement. "Aaron, there are dozens of men down there." She pointed to the wooded area.

Aaron banked quickly to the left and opened fire.

"Call them off," Liz ordered Kalel while shoving the weapon against his temple.

He simply smiled at her. "Why would I do that? You're outmanned."

"Because if they kill us, you'll die too," she told him.

Kalel shrugged. "But we'll take out two of the enemy in the process. So what if I die."

The man seated next to Kalel wasn't nearly as convinced. "Do as they ask. If we die here our story dies with us."

Aaron continued shooting, but the chopper was taking on heavy fire.

"We're going to have to get out of here," Aaron said. "We're outgunned."

Aaron continued shooting rounds as they prepared to leave. Over the tree tops three choppers appeared and Liz's heart sank.

She noticed Kalel looking out at them too. He wasn't relieved to see them.

"They're ours," Aaron shouted enthusiastically.

And Liz had never been so happy to see anyone in all her life.

The three Scorpion choppers came in firing heavily.

Aaron grabbed the mic. "Jase, it's me in the chopper. Don't shoot."

"Aaron?" Jase's shocked voice came through the mic. "What's going on?"

"You have enemy troops on the ground in the woods close to the cabin."

Right away, the three choppers zeroed in on the wooded area and began firing.

"Drop your weapons and come out into the clearing if you want to live," Jase announced on the loudspeaker over the noise of shooting.

Soon men began to emerge from the woods with their hands in the air.

Jase and the rest of the choppers landed in the clearing and immediately the Scorpions exited with weapons drawn.

"We have a man injured on board," Aaron told his team.

"Once you land, I'll send Ryan Samuels over to help him," Jase assured him.

Aaron found a safe landing place a little ways from the other machines. Ryan was ready and waiting as Aaron killed the chopper. He helped Davis disembark.

"I've got him." Ryan took the visibly weak Davis and headed for the cabin amongst ensuing chaos.

Aaron exited the chopper and waited as the man with Kalel got out of the chopper.

"You're next, Kalel," Liz said and kept her weapon trained on the man. Kalel cast her an angry look before he hopped from the chopper.

Aaron reached for the man. Kalel quickly jerked out of his reach, pulled a hidden gun from behind his back and fired dead-on.

EIGHTEEN

"Aaron!" Her heart leaped to her throat as Aaron's face contorted in pain and he stumbled backward then fell to the cold ground.

With the noise of the shot still ringing in her ears, Liz fired. The gun Kalel had used to wound Aaron flew from his hand. Someone charged Kalel, taking him down.

All Liz could think about was Aaron. She knelt next to him. The bullet had sliced clean through the right side of his body. He was unconscious.

"Hang on, Aaron," she begged him.

Please, God. Don't let him die.

"Somebody…please, I need help," she yelled, then took off her jacket and placed it over the wound, applying pressure.

Agent Ryan Samuels was the first to reach her. Ryan was a trained paramedic. "Let me take a look," he told her and gently pushed her hand away.

"Is he going to be okay?" she asked and hovered close. "Please, Ryan, don't let him die."

Ryan didn't answer. That alone was terrifying.

"Ryan," she pleaded for him to say something.

"I don't know. We need to get him inside right away." Agent Gavin Dalton appeared and the two men lifted Aaron and rushed him inside the cabin.

"There's a bedroom at the back of the cabin," Liz told them and they carried him to the room and laid him on the bed.

She stood close by; she wasn't about to leave his side, as Ryan ripped away Aaron's shirt to get a better view of the injury.

"It looks like a clean shot. The bullet exited straight through," Ryan told her and looked her in the eyes. "Liz, I need to stop the bleeding. Step outside and give me room."

She was about to refuse when Jase came over to her. "Let them work, Liz. Aaron's strong. If anyone can pull through this, it's him."

Jase was right. She slowly followed him out the door. She was crying and she didn't care.

"I want to say a prayer for him. Is that okay?" Jase asked.

She stared up at Jase. For a moment, she'd forgotten how close the two men were.

She nodded and wiped her eyes. "Yes, let's pray," she said gratefully.

Liz bowed her head as Jase prayed for Aaron. "Lord, our friend needs Your healing. Please guide Ryan's hands and keep Aaron strong... Amen."

Humbled by Jase's prayer, she whispered. "Thank you."

He squeezed her shoulder. "He's like a brother. I can see you care about him as well."

She shoved aside her fears. She loved Aaron and she didn't care who knew. "I do."

"You know, my wife always said the two of you would make the perfect couple," Jase said with a smile.

Kalel was restrained to a chair in the corner. "You think he'll talk? Or will he be like Sam?"

Jase shook his head. "No, I have a feeling he'll talk. He wants the world to know why he did the things he did."

She hoped Jase was right. Feeling completely helpless, Liz knew that the best way she could help Aaron was to find out what had truly happened to the evidence and the weapons.

Davis came over to where they stood watching as Gavin started interrogating Kalel. She noticed the fresh bandage covering Davis's wound.

"Jase, this is Davis Kincaid... Michael's brother." She made the introductions.

Jase couldn't even begin to hide his surprise. "I had no idea Michael even had a brother."

In all the chaos that had taken place, something occurred to Liz. Davis didn't seem surprised to hear Kalel had killed his brother.

"You knew Michael was dead before Kalel told you? How?" she asked in amazement.

Davis closed his eyes briefly. "You told me," he said and she stared at him without understanding. "I was the one who texted you the warning, at Michael's request. I didn't know Michael had died until then. You were the one who told me my brother was dead."

Liz was incapable of speaking, stunned by what Davis said.

"I think you'd better explain," Jase said for them both.

Davis slowly nodded. "The night he died, my brother called me and told me everything about his involvement with Kalel."

"Kalel? Michael was working for Kalel, not Sam?" Jase asked, but what he said didn't really surprise Liz.

Davis looked at him strangely. "Michael was never involved with Sam, but he wanted him to think he was. You see, Sam was always a loose cannon. Michael said Kalel blackmailed him into working for him so that he could keep an eye on Sam. Kalel even put his own brother inside Sam's organization to insure Sam did what he wanted."

Only it hadn't worked out that way. Sam had murdered Alhasan.

So many questions raced through Liz's mind. Davis seemed to intercept her questions. "Michael told me that Kalel had something on him, something that would ruin him if it was made known to the CIA."

Liz couldn't imagine what would be the tipping point from protecting your country to betraying it.

"Michael told me to warn Liz and he explained where he'd hidden the evidence that would clear her name and hopefully explain everything."

"You have the box," Liz supplied.

Davis smiled. "I do. I got to the cabin the day before I ran into you two. I found the box and managed to get it safely out of the cabin. That's why it took me so long to get back to you today. I had to move the evidence again. I was worried with all these men searching the area, they'd come upon my camp and find it."

"And the weapons?" Jase asked.

"Not here," Davis told them. "Michael knew that Kalel had something deadly planned for them and he couldn't live with himself if he let the weapons go, so he had them rerouted."

Liz's head reeled with all the new information. "Where are they?"

"He had his former marine buddy divert them to the Amish community near Eagle's Nest, Montana, where Michael and I were originally from."

She thought about the photo of Michael with another marine. Then something Kalel said made her ask, "You were once Amish?"

Davis smiled sympathetically. "At one time. I haven't been back there in years, but I think I would like to take Michael home." She could see it was hard for him to speak for a moment.

Davis drew in a breath. "Michael told me the weapons are in an old mine shaft near Eagle's Nest. I can help you find them."

Liz blew out a sigh. "Have you seen what's in the box?" She had to know what Michael had died to protect.

"I have. It's filled with years of evidence Michael accumulated. His personal ties to the Safar brothers and to Sam allowed him to gather enough proof to condemn Sam for weapons smuggling, and tie Kalel to numerous terrorist attacks throughout the world."

Jase shook his head in in disbelief. "What did Kalel have on Michael?"

"It wasn't so much what as who. Kalel threatened to kill Michael's mother, my stepmother. When he found out Michael had joined the CIA, he demanded that he find a way to join the Scorpion team. He said if he didn't he'd kill Rachel. Kalel told him he had people watching her all the time. He'd know if Michael tried to warn her." Davis shook his head. "I guess Michael believed him. I just wish he'd come to me sooner. I could have helped him." Davis's pain was clear. He felt as if he'd let his brother down. She understood the feeling all too well.

She touched his arm. "What happened isn't your fault. You did everything you could."

As relieved as she was that she was now in the clear, she couldn't enjoy the moment. All she could think about was Aaron. She was going out of her mind with worry. Ryan had been in there for a long time. Had something happened? She had to know.

Liz headed for the bedroom, when Ryan stepped out into the hall.

"Is he okay?" she asked before he'd managed even a single step.

Ryan grinned and some of her fear disappeared. "He is. He's awake and threatening to get out of bed if I don't get you…" She didn't let him finish.

She opened the door and ran to Aaron's bedside. The sight of the blood-soaked bandage on the man who had stood by her through all the dark moments they'd faced together was too much. She lost it. With tears streaming down her face she sat down next to him and hugged him tight.

Liz felt him wince and she jerked away and looked into his handsome face. "I'm sorry. Are you okay? Did I hurt you?"

He managed a smile and everything in the world righted itself. "I'm more than okay. I'm blessed."

Aaron pulled her back against him, ignoring the pain. He wanted her close, because he was so afraid he was dreaming. He'd handle a little discomfort.

"Is it over?" he asked and she knew what he meant.

She nodded against his chest. "It is." She told him everything Davis had said.

"Amazing," he said, unable to wrap his head around what had happened in such a short amount of time.

"How are you?" he asked, because he'd been so worried about her.

She pulled away so that she could look into his eyes. He saw all the love she felt for him shining in hers. "I'm going to be just fine."

Someone knocked on the door and Jase stepped inside and came over to the bed.

"Glad to see you upright, my friend," he said, and Aaron laughed then winced at the pain.

"Me too." Aaron managed.

"The state troopers are here. Ryan is going to transport you to the hospital in Anchorage just to be safe, but I wanted to tell you there's been a new development with Kalel," Jase told them.

He had Aaron's full attention. "What happened?" It couldn't be bad because Jase was smiling.

"Kalel's talking. It will take a while to get the whole story out of him, but apparently before he and his brother came to America, his family was killed in an attack on a village in Afghanistan. The attack was led by some of the original Scorpions."

"You're kidding," Aaron said in amazement.

Jase shook his head. "Nope. His uncle was a well-known terrorist responsible for several attacks on our team. Turns out the uncle escaped the village before our men arrived. Kalel and his brother were teenagers when they moved to Alaska to live with some distant relatives."

Aaron shook his head.

"That's when the brothers and Sam met," Jase said. "He introduced them to Michael. Through the years they kept in touch. Sam started his business as a cover to smuggle the weapons, only he got reckless. Kalel told him to find out where the Scorpions were headquartered and get rid of any evidence connecting Sam and the brothers to Michael. By that point, Kalel had decided Michael had to die. Of course, Sam failed miserably and ended up being captured."

Aaron couldn't believe what he was hearing. "He must have realized at some point we would dig deep enough to find his and Alhasan's connection to Sam and Michael."

Jase nodded. "That'd be my guess." He glanced at Liz. "Either way, this is over. You're cleared, Liz. Not that any of us believed you were guilty." He headed for the door then turned back to them. "You both need to get some rest on the way to Anchorage. We'll need both of you operating at full capacity to unravel the rest of Kalel's crimes."

Liz waited until they were alone again. "I still can't believe Michael would betray us like that. I wish he'd come to me and told me what was happening to him. I could have helped him."

Aaron drew her into the shelter of his arms. "He tried to redeem himself. Michael made sure that everyone knew you had nothing to do with his crimes and in the end he tried to right the wrongs he'd done."

"Do you think Kalel killed Sam too?" Liz asked, still trying to fit the pieces together.

"Probably. We know he killed Michael. I'm guessing he had Michael take your passkey, but I'm sure your partner never imagined that would lead to his own death. That Kalel would take your backup weapon to kill Michael and then frame you for the crime."

As hard as it was to believe, the team could finally close the book on Sam's dreadful story of terror once and for all.

Aaron just wished he could erase the moments of doubt he'd had about Liz. He should have trusted her completely.

"It's okay," she said softly and he looked into her eyes and shook his head.

"I doubted you. I can't believe I doubted your innocence for a second. You would never have done that to me. I'm not sure I can forgive myself," he muttered.

She clasped his chin and forced him to look at her. "No...you're wrong. If the tables were turned, I would have had doubts. We're only human, Aaron."

She smiled into his eyes. "None of that matters anymore. I love you, Aaron. After I lost Eric, I never thought I'd feel this way again. And if we hadn't gone through what we did, who knows, I might still be holding onto my grief. So, you see, everything worked out according to God's plan. I love you, Aaron," she said and he believed she meant it.

Tears stung his eyes and he gathered her closer and kissed her with all the love in his heart. "I love you too. And I promise I'm going to do whatever it takes never to doubt you again."

She touched her finger to his lips and shook her head. Then she kissed him and held him tight. "If there's one thing I've learned through all of this, it's that life is fragile. A precious gift from God and we're here for just a moment. I don't want to waste another minute of the time we have left on regrets. I want you. I want to spend the rest of our lives together and live each moment of that time to its fullest."

And so did Aaron. They'd been given a second chance at love. There had been a few bumpy patches leading to this moment, and many doubts, but they finally had a chance to explore the future together without anything hanging over their heads and he was so ready to take that chance with her.

* * * * *

If you enjoyed this book,
don't miss these other exciting stories
from Mary Alford:

FORGOTTEN PAST
ROCKY MOUNTAIN PURSUIT
DEADLY MEMORIES

Available now from Love Inspired Suspense!

Find more great reads at
www.LoveInspired.com

Dear Reader,

Where do you turn when your back is against the wall? When life is going our way, it's an easy question to answer. But what if you were being blamed for something you didn't do? In times of crisis, that's when our faith is tested.

This is the story behind my latest Love Inspired Suspense. For Agent Liz Ramirez, her faith in God has always proved unshakable, even after the death of her husband. Yet her faith in man is challenged when Liz is blamed for her partner's death. Facing prison time, she turns to the one person who has never once let her down. Agent Aaron Foster.

Liz is forced to go against the principles she's believed in since joining the Scorpions to find the evidence her deceased partner left behind in a remote cabin in Alaska. Evidence that will hopefully clear her name.

When everything points to Liz's guilt, Aaron willingly lays his life on the line to save hers.

And when everything is going against us, like it was for Liz, it would be so easy to give up. But it is in our darkest moments that God's light shines the brightest. And if we let Him, He'll be there beside us, no matter what. Just like Aaron was for Liz.

All the best...
Mary Alford

Get 2 Free Books,
Plus 2 Free Gifts—
just for trying the Reader Service!

Get 2 Free Books,

HARLEQUIN
HEARTWARMING™

Plus 2 Free Gifts—
just for trying the
Reader Service!

HOMETOWN HEARTS ♥

YES! Please send me **The Hometown Hearts Collection** in Larger Print. This collection begins with 3 FREE books and 2 FREE gifts in the first shipment. Along with my 3 free books, I'll also get the next 4 books from the Hometown Hearts Collection, in LARGER PRINT, which I may either return and owe nothing, or keep for the low price of $4.99 U.S./ $5.89 CDN each plus $2.99 for shipping and handling per shipment*. If I decide to continue, about once a month for 8 months I will get 6 or 7 more books, but will only need to pay for 4. That means 2 or 3 books in every shipment will be FREE! If I decide to keep the entire collection, I'll have paid for only 32 books because 19 books are FREE! I understand that accepting the 3 free books and gifts places me under no obligation to buy anything. I can always return a shipment and cancel at any time. My free books and gifts are mine to keep no matter what I decide.

262 HCN 3432 462 HCN 3432

Name	(PLEASE PRINT)	
Address		Apt. #
City	State/Prov.	Zip/Postal Code

Signature (if under 18, a parent or guardian must sign)

Mail to the **Reader Service:**

IN U.S.A.: P.O. Box 1867, Buffalo, NY. 14240-1867
IN CANADA: P.O. Box 609, Fort Erie, Ontario L2A 5X3

* Terms and prices subject to change without notice. Prices do not include applicable taxes. Sales tax applicable in NY. Canadian residents will be charged applicable taxes. This offer is limited to one order per household. All orders subject to approval. Credit or debit balances in a customer's account(s) may be offset by any other outstanding balance owed by or to the customer. Please allow 4 to 6 weeks for delivery. Offer available while quantities last. Offer not available to Quebec residents.

Your Privacy—The Reader Service is committed to protecting your privacy. Our Privacy Policy is available online at www.ReaderService.com or upon request from the Reader Service.

We make a portion of our mailing list available to reputable third parties that offer products we believe may interest you. If you prefer that we not exchange your name with third parties, or if you wish to clarify or modify your communication preferences, please visit us at www.ReaderService.com/consumerschoice or write to us at Reader Service Preference Service, P.O. Box 9062, Buffalo, NY. 14240-9062. Include your complete name and address.

HHBPA17